THE
SACRED
WHITE
TURKEY

Frances Washburn

♾

Publication of this volume was
assisted by the Virginia Faulkner
Fund, established in memory of
Virginia Faulkner, editor in chief
of the University of Nebraska Press.

Library of Congress
    Cataloging-in-Publication Data
Washburn, Frances.
    The sacred white turkey /
Frances Washburn.
    p. cm. — (Flyover fiction)
ISBN 978-0-8032-2846-7
    (paperback.: alkaline paper)
1. Women — Fiction. 2. Indians
    of North America — Fiction.
3. Shamans — Fiction. 4. Satire.
    I. Title.
PS3623.A8673S33 2010
    813'.6 — dc22   2009049903

Set in Monotype Dante.
Designed by A. SHAHAN.

For my children,
Lee & Stella,
who have the most
important quality
in the world.
They are decent
human beings.

THE
SACRED
WHITE
TURKEY

1 Stella

On easter Sunday in 1963, a white turkey appeared on Hazel Latour's doorstep, pecking at the door as if demanding entrance. That turkey set in motion a series of events that would rock the community from end to end, upset the established order, and make some of the most traditional among us question our beliefs. Had I not been there, I would not have believed what was to come, and even after all these years, I still doubt my own senses, wonder about where the turkey came from, why it came to my grandmother, of all people, and where it went. That white turkey was *wakan*, and you know, some of our people say that word means holy, and some say, no, it just means something unexplainable, and a lot of things can be unexplainable without being holy. Some people make jokes and say that the bia is *wakan* because nothing that bureaucracy does is explainable, and that makes the people who think the word means holy and sacred pretty mad. Disrespectful. Sacrilegious even, if you can apply *that* word to a belief system that isn't Christian. I believe the turkey was both holy and unexplainable. I've tried a thousand explanations over more than forty years for all the things that happened, and none of them make sense. I can't prove anything. I only know what

I saw, me, with my own two eyes. Once you've heard the story, you can believe it or not.

A gentle knocking more like a tapping awoke me from my dreams of candy eggs delivered by a pink bunny, even though I was twelve years old and knew better. Hazel was a medicine woman, which meant that people were likely to show up at any hour of day or night with a sick relative or an injured animal asking for her help. I thought sure that was what the tapping was. It was early, the sun barely up, so I knew Hazel would be down milking the cow, but I could open the door and make a welcome.

I leaped out of the heavy comforters and into the crispness of the spring morning, ran to the door, and there stood not a person but a white turkey, cocking its head from side to side, darting its beak at the cats that dared annoy it, and pecking at the door. I had heard that some people bought their children colored chicks for easter, but Hazel would never stoop to such foolishness, not when our own hens hatched out perfectly lovely yellow babies every spring; nor was there likely to be a basket of candy eggs hidden in the flour bin for me to find, and certainly she would not have gotten me a turkey for easter.

Hazel almost dropped the milk pail she was carrying up from the shed, where the cow stood outside the battered wooden door placidly chewing her cud.

"What's this?" she said to me, and then to the turkey, "And where did you come from?"

The turkey trotted over to her, sure the pails contained grain, but Hazel pushed the turkey away with her rubber-booted foot. It danced sideways, pecking at her boot.

"Hmm," she said with her brows lowered at me, standing there shivering in my skivvies. "Is this your doing, Stella?"

I shook my head.

"Strange timing. It's months and months until thanksgiving,"

Hazel said as she opened the door and deposited the pail of milk on the table. Outside the cats clawed at the screen, yowling, demanding their share of the fresh, steaming milk. The white turkey pecked at the cats, pecked at the screen.

"Grandma," I started, but no sooner was the word out of my mouth than her hand shot out and slapped me across the mouth hard enough to sting.

"The name is Hazel," she said, "even though I am a grandmother, yours." I did know better, but the appearance of the turkey had addled my brain, made me want some comfort, even if only in naming her as my grandmother.

Quickly, she pulled me to her cow-sweat-smelling shirt and hugged me so tight I could barely breathe.

"I love you more than life, little one," she said. "But I don't like to be reminded of—things." She held me a moment more, than pushed me toward the door. "Go get some oats for that turkey. No. Wait, get yourself dressed first."

I ran back to the bedroom, pulled on the knees-out jeans I had shed on the floor the night before, stomped my feet sockless into my old worn boots while pulling on an old blue checkered shirt of Hazel's that hung on me like a sack.

She was putting together the parts of the cream separator when I came back through the kitchen, glancing through the screen from time to time.

I hesitated.

"Hazel? Is it special?"

"Is what special?"

"The turkey. It's white. I've never seen a white turkey. Does that make it special? And it came on easter Sunday."

She was just sitting down on the bench with the cream separator mounted on it, ready to turn the crank. The corners of her mouth turned up in amusement.

"You mean some spiritual being?"

I nodded doubtfully, fiddling with a button on the baggy shirt.

"Don't be silly. It's just a turkey. It probably escaped from a truck going through on the highway or wandered off from somebody's place around here."

"But I never heard of anyone around here raising turkeys."

"Doesn't mean somebody hasn't just got a flock recently," she said, putting the steel bowl on top of the separator, laying the clean filter cloth over the top of that, fastening it on with clothes pins.

"And it's white," I said, "Aren't turkeys always brown or black? Like the ones we color in school at thanksgiving."

She shook her head.

"No, dear. These days turkey farmers breed for white ones. They're easier to clean for the market. Not so many pin-feathers."

Pinfeathers. I knew about those. Little feathers just emerging that had to be picked out of the chicken's skin when we dressed them, a tedious job, but not so nasty as having to kill the chickens and pull out the guts, saving back the liver, the gizzard, and the heart.

I heard the slow hum of the separator as Hazel started turning the crank.

The turkey picked at the oats I put out for it as if it was starving. It was a real creature, then; it had to eat, could not live off air, but I couldn't help noticing how very *white* and clean this turkey was. The chickens that we kept had dusty feathers in spite of constant preening and pecking to rid themselves of mites, and there were always traces of manure around their butts. This turkey looked as if it had been bathed in bleach water and polished with car wax. It gleamed.

When it had finished all the oats I had scattered for it, it strolled off as if taking a tour of the place. I followed it, half expecting it to speak to me, but of course, it only uttered the usual turkey nonsense. I thought that perhaps I had not the wisdom to understand whatever message it had. Maybe the message was not for me at all. At the chicken house, it stopped, looked inside, strolled in, promptly appropriating the end roost, the one that the black rooster had claimed as his territory. He did not object, but only gave a little dip of his head as he moved aside. In spite of Hazel's words, I believed that turkey was sent for a purpose, or was a spirit that had sent itself. More than forty years later, no matter what Hazel said, I still believe that or something like it even though I have no evidence to prove it.

School still had some weeks to run, and I was glad because all the students at the little county school lived so far apart that we didn't often see each other in the summer. I wanted to share my story of the coming of the white turkey, but when I breathlessly told the Morris sisters and Avril Lately, they only stared at me.

Finally, Teensy Morris said, "Oh, you're just making up stories again."

"I'm not! It's true! It's big and white and it's a turkey."

Avril gave a snort of disgust.

"Turkeys don't come in white. Everyone knows that."

"Yes, they do!" I said, hands on my hips ready to slap them into believing me. "Hazel said that farmers raise white ones 'cause they're easier to clean. You don't know everything!"

So it was that Teensy and Melva Morris and Avril Lately walked home from school with me, even though it was a mile in the wrong direction from their homes, to see the white turkey.

There it was, perched on the edge of the horse tank, getting a drink. I ran toward it in panic. What if it fell in and drowned? It happened to a chicken every now and then. But as I reached out to grab the turkey, I slipped in the muddy overflow from the tank and sprawled on my back, knocking the wind out of myself. As I lay there panting for breath, the turkey jumped down, squished through the mud, and stood by my face, where it bent its head to look at my eyes. For one moment I thought it would peck my eyes out for foolishly trying to grab it, but it only made a garbled cluck, cocked its head, and pecked at something in the mud beside my ear. I sat up.

The Morris sisters and Avril stood staring at the turkey, at me.

"See!" I gasped out. "I *told* you we had a white turkey."

"Wow," said Avril, and then, "Where did it come from?"

"Is it—is it—*wakan?*" Teensy asked in a soft, low voice.

There. That was the word I had been searching for.

"Yes," I said trying to look dignified and deserving of a sacred white turkey, standing there in my muddied clothes.

"Stella," my grandmother's voice came ominously from behind the kitchen screen door where I could barely see her for the glare of sun. I had been caught out running my mouth. Again.

Hazel opened the screen door and walked out onto the stone step, a dish towel in her hand. Her dark, gray shot hair gleamed in the setting sun, silhouetting her tall, slender figure, held erect in that posture I knew meant she was less than happy with me.

"Stella, don't be filling people's heads full of nonsense."

She sat down on the step, dish towel in her lap.

"Come here," she said, patting either side of her. The Morris sisters and Avril went reluctantly, Avril standing in front of her but well back out of her reach, Teensy and Melva gingerly sitting as if the step was hot. Hazel had a reputation, one that I think she liked to perpetrate. She was a healer and a good one: sometimes her cures were so immediate, so long-lasting, that people talked. They said that anyone that effective had to be in touch with more than just the good spirits. It didn't help that Hazel still looked young in her mid-forties, still beautiful, still turned the heads of men, including the heads of those who gossiped. The biggest talker of all was not a woman, but a man, George Wanbli, a big voiced medicine man from up on Potato Creek. He scoffed at everything good said about Hazel. He was jealous of her, I know now. Medicine men don't charge for their services, exactly, but it is traditional of people seeking their help to bring a gift along with the request for help. Sometimes, they bring money, but usually the gift is more tangible—always an offering of tobacco, but also coffee, sugar, a case of soda or two or something like. Medicine people are supposed to go into the profession because they feel called to help others, because they have a connection with the spirit world, not because of what presents in money or goods they can extract from people. I don't know any rich medicine people, but some have more than others. George Wanbli had an active practice, with more people coming to see him than any other *wicasa waken* on the rez, but he was a jealous man who didn't want to be shown up by any other medicine person, especially not Hazel. She was a woman for one thing, and women *wicasa wakan* were not usual among us Lakota. Besides that, Hazel was gaining a reputation that made George feel threatened. Medicine people may have better contacts with the spirits, but they aren't always wise people, or even kind.

"Stella, you too," Hazel said.

I walked over beside her just as reluctantly as the other kids, but not because I was afraid of Hazel's powers, not spiritual ones anyway, but the power of her right hand to swat me for showing out.

"Listen to me!" Hazel said. "That turkey is just a bird. It is NOT *wakan*. An eagle may be holy, or a certain place on the earth where a wonderful thing happened." She nodded toward the turkey, now pecking small stones from the ground. "Look at it. It's a bird, a domesticated one at that. Turkeys are stupid birds. They say that in a rainstorm, turkeys will drown because they don't have sense enough to keep their heads down so water doesn't run up their noses. That's probably not true, but they can't be smart or they wouldn't have gotten lulled into eating what people give them, sticking around until they're fat and we chop their heads off and eat them for thanksgiving dinner. See?"

Avril nodded, but his eyes kept returning to the turkey.

"See? You hear what I say?" Hazel looked from one Morris sister to the other. They nodded their heads vigorously. Hazel put her hands on the backs of their necks and pulled them up as she stood. "IT'S JUST A TURKEY. Now, go home. Your mommas will be wondering why you're so late."

She stood there looking after them as they walked back up the lane from our house heading home, lunch pails bumping against their thighs.

"Bye!" I yelled after them, but only Melva had nerve enough to give a little waggle of her hand.

"Stella."

I didn't want to look up.

"You can't be starting rumors about a dumb barnyard animal being a holy creature. It's not. You know that."

I didn't know any such of thing, but I couldn't say that to Hazel, so I didn't say anything.

"We'll have half the countryside out here to see this damned turkey, if rumors get started."

"I didn't start any rumors!" I protested. "Teensy is the one who said it was *wakan*."

"Then you should have told her that it isn't *wakan*. If it happens again, you know what to say?"

"Yes, Hazel. It's just a turkey. A dumb domesticated bird."

"Right."

Half the countryside started showing up that very night. After supper, a car drove into the yard, and more than half a dozen people stepped out. Avril's parents, his grandmother who lived with them, his three younger brothers, and older sister, Nancy, who had always tormented me in school before she graduated and went on to high school last year. Mrs. Lately had her arms full of bags.

"I've brought some clothes of Nancy's that she's outgrown," Mrs. Lately said as Hazel came out to greet them. "I thought Stella might get some good out of them. I hate to throw out anything good."

Hazel took the bags with a smile and a thank you, but I knew I would never wear any of those clothes. Hazel said that Clara Lately let Nancy dress like a hooker. One of her skirts wouldn't make a good-sized dish rag.

"Come in," Hazel said. "I've got coffee on the stove and half a batch of cream puffs."

I wished Hazel hadn't said that. I loved cream puffs, but Hazel didn't make them very often. She saved every ounce of cream to sell in town to pay for coffee, sugar, flour, and an occasional package of hamburger, ground fresh at Jerry's Market. I knew there wouldn't be any cream puffs left after Clara Lately and her family left. Clara was the joke of every gathering, funeral, wedding, ceremony, or whatever. People said she always left with a doughnut stuck on every finger, and it wasn't far from the truth. She would displace a lot of water if she could be fully submerged, a concept I had just learned in school.

"Let's go see the turkey," Avril whispered.

"Yeah, let's!" his youngest brother, Lester, insisted.

"I don't know," I said. "Hazel's mad at me about showing off the turkey." I turned and went into the house behind their father, Ed, a skinny little man who looked like he didn't get enough to eat.

They sat at the table while Clara Lately removed every piece of clothing from the bags, one at a time, and held them up to me. I was six inches shorter than Nancy Lately. Most of the pieces had seen better days, with frayed hems and stains from who knew what. One white sundress had grass stains on the back. Grandmother Lately fingered the fabric of the various items and remarked that they would have made good material for the quilt she was making.

I was tired of the Latelys long before they were ready to go home. They lingered over cup after cup of coffee and just one more of those cream puffs, "Hazel, you're such a good baker." Finally, even Clara couldn't think of another thing to say, so she just came out with it.

"Avril says you've got a turkey. A *white* turkey."

Hazel shot me a look from her black eyes that said "YOU!"

I changed my mind. The longer the Latelys stayed, the more time Hazel had to get over being mad at me for telling about the turkey.

"We had one wander in here on Sunday morning," she said. "I'm going to put an ad in the paper about it. It belongs to someone, that's sure. It's been well fed."

Clara licked a spot of cream off the back of her hand.

"We've never seen a live turkey before," Clara said. "I can't imagine a *white* turkey."

Hazel shrugged.

"It's just an ordinary turkey, except it's white."

"Grandma," Clara said, poking the old lady awake. "Grandma, have you ever seen a turkey before?"

The old lady's milky cataract eyes stared at the corner of the ceiling.

"No. I can't recall ever seeing one. A live one, that is. But I've seen many a cooked one. Did I tell you about—"

Clara smoothly interrupted.

"It would really be nice if Grandma could see a real live turkey," Clara said. "She's not getting any younger, you know."

I wondered how she could see the turkey anyway with her eyes half blinded with cataracts.

"Avril saw the turkey!" Avril's next-youngest brother, Melvin, spoke up now from his position beside his grandmother, where he had been silently pinching off bites of the last cream puff, which she had in front of her but couldn't seem to find with her gnarled, arthritic hands.

"It's just a turkey," Hazel said, "a dumb animal." The way she was looking at Clara, I wondered who she thought was a dumb animal.

Mr. Lately spoke up. "Are you *sure* it was a turkey, Avril? Might have been a white wild goose or—"

"It's a turkey!" Hazel said. "All right. Everybody out. We're going to see the turkey."

She grabbed the flashlight from atop the refrigerator and led the way out the front door to the chicken coop. Clara rushed after, leaving her husband to lead Grandma stumbling along behind as she tried to shake off Mr. Lately's hand.

"I'm old and half blind," she grumbled. "I'm not a cripple."

The flashlight beam bounced along the weed-bordered path as Hazel took long strides. One of the kids tripped over a sleepy cat, came out to see what the fuss was about. The cat yowled and ran off into the weeds.

Hazel waited until the entire Lately family clustered at the chicken coop door, and then she ceremoniously pulled out the stick that went through the hasp to keep the door shut.

"Be quiet," she said. "No use disturbing the hens."

The moon was just rising over the distant hills, a fat spring moon that made the flashlight unnecessary for seeing outside once your eyes got used to the semi-light.

Hazel opened the door and aimed the flashlight inside the coop, motioning the Latelys one at a time to step up and peek through. Avril pushed his way to the front, but Melvin jerked him back.

"Not you! You already saw!"

Clara pushed them both aside and leaned over slightly to peer through the low door.

"I see chickens," she said.

"Of course you do," Hazel said. "It's a hen house."

"But where's the turkey?" Clara's voice was muffled as she pushed her round body through the shorter than normal door.

"Look at the end roost," Hazel said.

"I don't see . . ." Clara started to say.

A fluttering of heavy wings interrupted her, and a loud sound that wasn't exactly a gobble, wasn't exactly a squawk, wasn't anything human, either. It came from behind them, from the fence that divided the chicken pen from the cow pen, and all the Latelys pushed forward against each other, shoving Clara to her knees in the mess on the floor of the chicken coop.

I turned, and there with the moon behind its head like a halo sat the white turkey, with something around its head like a shiny crown of thorns. Again came that sound, "RRR ppptt." I never heard a turkey make that sound before or since, but there was no doubt it came from the turkey's beak, directly from the turkey's beak, a pronouncement on the state of affairs it observed.

Old Grandma Lately saw—well, whatever it was that a half-blind old lady could see, or thought she saw.

"*Wakan!*" she exclaimed. "It's holy! Look, it has a halo! And a crown of thorns! And it said 'REPENT'!"

It didn't sound like "repent" to me, more like it had a piece of corn caught in its craw.

"It's not *wakan!*" Hazel yelled. "It's just a goddamned turkey, for chrissake!"

Clara had backed out of the chicken house on all fours, looked over her shoulder, and saw the turkey perched on the fence with the halo of the moon behind it, and immediately rose to her knees and began praying the Hail Mary, but she couldn't remember the words past the first line, so she only repeated it louder.

"Hail Mary, full of . . . full of . . . Hail Mary, full of . . . HAIL MARY, FULL OF . . . ," as she reached out and pulled the Old Lady down to her knees, too.

The rest of the family stood shocked, staring back and forth between the turkey and the kneeling women.

Then Mr. Lately hollered, "It's a sign! A sign from the spirits," and he began a prayer in Lakota. "Tunkasila . . ."

"STOP IT!" Hazel yelled and began laying about her with the flashlight, one blow catching Clara alongside the head, after which she toppled over moaning into the weeds. Another near blow brought the turkey down off the fence, where it gave a very normal turkey sounding "gobblegobblegobble" and walked sedately into the chicken coop.

It took half an hour to herd the hysterical Latelys back to the house, and another pot of coffee and another hour of talking from Hazel before they seemed calm enough to drive safely home, Clara with a wet dishcloth pressed to the knot on her forehead. But Hazel was not able to convince them that they had not seen something out of the ordinary. After that, Hazel was too tired to take me to task for telling Avril about the turkey. We just went to bed.

The next morning when I went out to feed the chickens—and the turkey—I saw that the turkey had gotten an old piece of barbed wire wrapped around its head and neck that it couldn't get off, or maybe didn't want to get off. I pushed the turkey up in the corner of the hen house and pulled the wire off, leaving a few little drops of red on the turkey's neck where the barbs had pierced. I showed it to Hazel, and she just shook her head.

"Fools will believe anything," she said.

That very day she went to town and put an ad in the LOST, STRAYED, STOLEN section of the newspaper Want Ads. It read: "Strayed in to Hazel Latour's place, one white turkey. Will the owner please claim it."

No one did, but the ad sure stirred up conversation. There were no turkey farmers within five hundred miles or more, no turkey processing plants any closer than Minnesota. Highway 20 ran along just south of the state line, but it wasn't the main route for trucks to take when transporting turkeys to the slaughter plants. The railroad tracks paralleled the highway, but the trains didn't transport poultry either, or not that anybody could swear to. Speculation said that maybe a truck had gotten off its main route and come through on the highway; maybe the turkey had escaped from a cage that way. But wouldn't the turkey have been injured crawling out of a wire cage and falling off a truck going at least fifty miles an hour? Then someone else wondered, how could that turkey have made its way across twenty miles of prairie with no water and nothing to eat and coyotes running around out there, not to mention the occasional farm or ranch dog? It might not be a holy turkey, but its appearance was certainly strange and unexplainable.

Hazel decided to put another ad in a paper in the next town over, but the results were the same: no results except for more talk. We would wait a little longer, she decided, and then we would have turkey for dinner, maybe for memorial day, or fourth of July at the latest.

I begged her not to kill the turkey. It might be bad luck, I said, but she laughed at me and told me not to listen to idle talk. In the end, it wasn't my begging that saved the turkey, it was Hazel's own practical ways.

After the Latelys began spreading the story of the turkey's miraculous appearance, other people began showing up. I think they were afraid of the turkey, didn't necessarily want a visitation of the spirit within it but wanted to satisfy some curiosity with a sighting from a distance—in the daytime, of course. People that used to take their troubles to George Wanbli or one of the other *wicasa wakan* started bringing their offerings of tobacco and money, bags of sugar and three-pound cans of Folgers to Hazel.

A car or a pickup would drive up, people would get out with bags of goods. They would observe the social graces of chatting over a cup of coffee and then present their tobacco and gifts and ask Hazel if she would help them with their problem. She could refuse, or she could agree, but if it seemed a worthy case, she agreed. People rarely came to a medicine man with a foolish request; they knew better. Even if a medicine person agreed to take the case, the spirits would likely be annoyed and give a bad outcome. Hazel's supplicants were real, all right, but while they were getting out of the car, while they were presenting their case, or while they were leaving, they were looking out of the corners of their eyes for a glimpse of the turkey. I knew Hazel was annoyed, she talked about it to me, but she also knew that most of the people had a legitimate need for help, so she wouldn't turn them down just because they had some silly notion that a turkey could be sacred.

A little cash money came in, but much more goods. Our cabinets were full for the first time I could ever remember, with more piled on top. There were stacks of cans full of coffee, cases of canned vegetables, fruit, soup, and bags of sugar that Hazel finally had to put into a metal trash can with a tight lid to keep the ants out of it. Our refrigerator had so much meat inside that Hazel had to rent a cold storage locker in town to preserve the meat that we couldn't eat up right away. I never felt so full when I left the table, so rich.

The house smelled, too, not just of cooking food, but of the cedar, sage, and sweetgrass that Hazel burned as part of the ceremonies she performed for her clients. They worked, too, almost every time, and that brought those people back when they had other problems, brought other people who heard of Hazel's success. It was a prosperous time, and Hazel knew it was because of the white turkey.

One day coming back from a trip to deposit yet more meat in the cold storage locker in town, she brought up the subject of the turkey dinner.

"I don't want you to get the wrong idea," she began, "because that turkey is NOT *wakan*. It is just a turkey, a bird. It's true that it's because of the turkey that we have more now than we ever had before, but it's just circumstances because silly people choose to believe in something even sillier than themselves. There's a logical explanation for where that turkey came from, even if we don't know what it is. You understand?"

I did understand. I knew she was feeling guilty about using the turkey as a drawing card for her medicine man practice.

"We're going to eat that turkey," she said, "but not just yet."

"Okay," I said, and pulled back as she reached out and tugged on my pony tail.

Hazel was wrong about the sacredness of the white turkey, but I couldn't tell her why. She would never have believed me. The white turkey was *wakan*, but not because of some piece of barbed wire wrapped around its head, not because some people thought it spoke to them. On the night the turkey had appeared on the fence to the Latelys, I had put it up for the night with the chickens. The turkey was inside on the end roost where the black rooster used to sit. I saw it there, gleaming in the muted light as I shut the door and put the wooden pin through the hasp on the door. That chicken coop was animal proof. Hazel had made it so after losing too many chickens to winter hungry coyotes, and I had helped her nail strips of board over every crack. That turkey could not have escaped to sit on the fence in the moonlight under any ordinary circumstances, but it had.

That was the first miracle of the white turkey. There would be more.

2 Stella

Five weeks after the white turkey appeared on Hazel Latour's doorstep, it laid an egg. It had probably learned from our chickens, the sneaky rogues. We had nests of straw in the chicken house for them to lay their eggs in, but they had free run of the place, so some of them laid eggs outside in the weeds around the old fallen-down barn, behind the outhouse, under the porch. Sneaky they might be, but not very smart, because no hen can resist announcing the birth of an egg to the entire world. We listened and tracked down the eggs. Once in a great while a smarter hen managed to keep her beak shut or her voice low enough so we didn't hear, or waited until we were gone to pop out an egg and announce it. Then, on a day when we weren't expecting anything special, a hen would come clucking and shepherding chicks into the yard, showing off to Hazel and me, sometimes just two or three little yellow fuzz balls coaxed along behind their mother, sometimes ten or more that she had to keep from getting lost in the weeds.

It was my job to find the hidden eggs, and one day while I was looking under some old boards behind the cow shed, I found another nest with a bigger egg, brown and freckled as a redheaded child. I'd seen big hen eggs; those with a double yoke are usually bigger, but this one would have held quadruplets if it had been a chicken egg, and I knew that was impossible. This egg would have to have been delivered from a chicken by Caesarian section, although I didn't know of that human reproductive procedure at the time. I did know this was no hen egg, so it had to be a turkey egg. I fetched Hazel.

We kneeled as we peered under a board at the egg, lit by a little shaft of sunlight through a knothole.

Hazel sat up and said, "Yes. It's a turkey egg."

I waited for her to go on, looking at her.

"It's a turkey egg, so we know it's a hen," she continued, as if she hadn't known all along that it was a hen.

I knew about animal reproduction; you can't grow up on a farm without knowing those things, about how animals get made and how they get born.

"But," I said.

"But what? There isn't a male turkey around to be the father? There doesn't have to be a male turkey for our hen to lay an egg. This one might be just an egg, you know. Unfertilized. An egg with no baby turkey inside, just goop."

I must have looked puzzled.

She flung her arms up and slapped them down on her thighs.

"Stella! You know, sometimes we crack open an egg to fry and there's a blood spot inside? That's because it's fertile. The blood spot is the beginning of a baby chick. If we had let the hen keep it and sit on it, it would have hatched a chick. But hens lay eggs whether or not there is a rooster around, and so do turkeys. Those unfertilized ones just won't hatch out a baby. Do you see?"

I fiddled with the raveled edge of my shirt sleeve, unwilling to meet Hazel's annoyed eyes.

"But how come she didn't lay any eggs until now?"

"*Anogoptanpe*," Hazel said and settled down among the weeds and the old boards, careful to avoid the rusty nails sticking out of them. "Chickens and turkeys have to have food and water in order to make eggs. If they don't have much food for a while, their bodies stop making eggs. They still have the beginnings of eggs, and when they have food again, after a while those eggs mature and the chicken or the turkey lays them. It's not mysterious. This egg is not fertile. You understand? It won't hatch out into a baby."

I nodded. "Yes. It's just a regular old egg, and if nobody ate it, it would go rotten."

I loved finding a nest of rotten eggs, unfertilized ones that the hen who laid them had abandoned perhaps from some instinctual knowledge that they wouldn't hatch. The best thing about a nest of rotten eggs was getting to smash them, throwing them up against the big square post at the end of the cow pen, watching the stinky yellow-green mess run down the post. It was disgustingly fun. Even better was a rotten egg fight. I did that only once with Avril and his brothers, Melvin and Norris and Lester, and it was a wonderful memory, except for the part when Hazel found out and gave me the one spanking I had ever gotten. You can't hide the smell and the slime of rotten eggs on your clothes no matter how many times you swish them in the horse tank water.

"Are we going to eat this egg?" I asked.

"What do you think we should do?"

"I kind of don't want to," I said.

"Why not? It's an egg, just a little bigger than a chicken egg. One of these would do for a cake."

"Well, maybe in a cake where it's all mixed up with other things, so I didn't have to think about it," I said.

Hazel pushed a puff of air through her lips, a disgusted sound.

"It's an egg. Liquid chicken. Liquid turkey. Not any real difference." She thought a minute, and then she said, "Come to think of it, though, I guess it is pretty disgusting if you think about where it came from. I wonder about the first person who saw an egg coming out of chicken's behind and said, 'I think I'll eat that.'"

I giggled at that picture in my head. Then Hazel was laughing until we could hardly stop, sitting there beside the turkey nest.

Finally, stomach muscles hurting, I said to Hazel, "Can we just leave this egg for now?"

"Why?"

I didn't want to say why. I was afraid of Hazel's scorn, but I managed to say, "I just want to see what happens. Maybe there will be other eggs."

"As much grain as that turkey eats, there will be lots of other eggs. But if you think it's going to hatch, you're being as silly as all the other fools around here. There isn't any male turkey to father chicks. You know that."

"Yes," I nodded. "But I don't want to eat it. Not even in a cake."

Hazel lowered her head and looked at me under her brows.

"Nice big eggs like this, though, they would make a big stink in a rotten egg smash, wouldn't they?" she said.

I couldn't look at her. She was silent, and I could feel her eyes upon the top of my own lowered head.

"All right," she conceded. "But NO throwing them at Avril or anyone else. These are target practice only. Got that?"

I agreed.

School was out, and that meant not less work for me, but more. The garden had to be tended, the garden from which we would glean vegetables for our table—radishes, green leaf lettuce, and baby carrots to eat fresh, and later on tomatoes and cucumbers, corn and beans, for fresh eating and canning for winter. I spent hours on my knees crawling between the rows, pulling weeds and thinning the plants. Hazel was merciless in her inspections. Her sharp sight could spot a weed a quarter of an inch high with only two leaves clinging to a tiny stem.

Hazel busied herself with meeting people who came in ever increasing numbers asking for a ceremony for a sick relative, help for a child in trouble with the law, guidance for decisions on whether to move for an off-reservation job, which would mean a better standard of living but also leaving behind relatives, going to a place where one spoke Lakota, and no one understood the puns that were so commonly created between English and Lakota. Then there were the ceremonies themselves that Hazel performed for the petitioners, ceremonies where she sometimes let me assist in small ways like keeping the sweetgrass or sage burning by blowing on it while she recited her petition to the spirits, but more often, she would not let me observe.

More of the chores fell to me, besides my regular duties of weeding the garden and tending the chickens and the turkey. When I was much younger I had wanted to learn to milk the cow, but Hazel said, "No, if you learn to do something, you get stuck doing it," which seemed strange, but she told me that her uncle had taught her to milk cows, and after that, she had been expected to do it while the uncle went drinking late at night and slept in with his hangover the next day while Hazel milked the cow. But she was not her uncle, and there were only so many hours in the day, so now that I was older and did not care to learn, she taught me to milk. It was harder work than I bargained for because the cow was used to Hazel and hated me, taking every opportunity to slap me in the face with her green manure-crusted tail, to step on my foot, or kick at me under pretense of dislodging flies.

I took over the chore of separating the cream from the milk, too, harder work than it seemed because you had to lift the heavy bucket of milk up to pour into the bowl on top without spilling the milk and without pouring so fast that the rush of milk dislodged the clothes pins that held the straining cloth in place. The crank on the side took a while to get moving, too, as if it were reluctant to move, but once I got it spinning, momentum kept it going with little effort while the yellow cream dripped out of one spout into a clean stainless steel can, then saved up daily to be sold in town, while the pale bluish-colored skimmed milk ran in a steady stream out another spout and into another pail, some to be used for cooking and drinking, but most to be poured over grain and fed to our two hogs.

In between the work, I stole moments to go look at the egg. I had no plans to smash it. I was convinced it held a baby turkey, no matter that I knew about turkey mating, that there was no rooster turkey to father babies. There would be a turkey inside, I was sure of it. Two days after the first egg, there was another, exactly the same as the first one. The turkey was sitting on the eggs now, leaving the nest only for brief moments in the morning when I put out the grain. I watched and chose those moments to peek into the nest. After two weeks, there were nine eggs, and then no more.

Hazel had an *Old Farmer's Almanac* with tables that told how long it took animals to have a baby. I already knew about cows; ours birthed a calf in a little over nine months. I remembered Hazel driving the cow across the back pasture and through the fence to the neighbor's bull, watching the courtship and the bull mounting the cow, and afterward marking the calendar so we would know when the calf would be born. Hazel planned the birth so it wouldn't happen in the early days of spring when the calf might die in the wet cold of a late snow storm. That had happened once, and we had brought the calf into the kitchen for a few days to keep it warm, fed it with a bottle of milk from its mother.

The almanac was Hazel's bible. There wasn't just one, either.

A new one came out every year, but Hazel kept the old ones together in chronological order. A new one would arrive in the mail, clean and smelling of ink, but as Hazel repeatedly consulted it for information on the weather and on planting times, and sometimes, I think, just to read the pithy sayings that were interspersed throughout the useful information, the pages became dog eared and ragged and stained with coffee. She kept them on top of the freestanding kitchen cupboard that held the dishes, and I was not to touch it.

I waited until Hazel went to town to sell the cream, pleading a stomach ache to stay behind. She was suspicious of that story because sometimes, not every time, she let me have a dime to spend on penny candy at Jackson's Five and Dime Store, a treat I loved, but she let me stay home anyway. I guess maybe she thought I was tired from doing most of the chores.

When the sound of the motor in Hazel's old pickup faded down the short lane to the main road, I pushed a chair up to the cupboard, reached on top, and brought down the stack of almanacs. I sat down at the oilcloth-covered kitchen table, still damp from wiping off after doing up the breakfast dishes, and spread the almanacs in an arc in front of me. They were thin, more like pamphlets than books. I knew that at least one of them would have what I was looking for—information on how long it took for a turkey to hatch out her eggs. I thumbed through them, and found tables in the back of the latest edition—gestational tables—they were called, or incubation times—for a whole variety of farm animals from cows to ducks. I ran my ragged fingernail down the column to turkey: twenty-eight days. Four weeks. About one month. I got the calendar down from its nail on the wall, the one sent out free from the feed mill in town the previous December, and tried to remember the exact date I had found the first egg. A little thinking got me a date: April 28, and a little more math gave me May 26 as the day the first egg would be likely to hatch. I sat and figured some more and decided that the last egg could hatch as late as June 10. After the first one hatched, the turkey would do what the chicken hens did—sit on the nest to keep the rest of the eggs warm while simultaneously trying to keep the already hatched ones from straying far from her where they could get lost and starve or get eaten by the cats. That had to be a difficult job, I thought. I was glad I wasn't a chicken. Then I thought it might not be so bad because at least the length of time it took to do that was short, while humans—from the time a human baby was born until it was grown was years, years of work and worry. I didn't think I wanted to have babies. I would prefer to have chickens. Or turkeys.

Someone pounded on the front screen door, rattling it as if to knock it from its shaky hinges. I jumped as if I had been shot, tried to gather the almanacs into a pile and only succeeded in knocking several onto the floor and creasing the cover of one. From where I sat at the table, I could see only a shadow against the screen. I should have spoken out immediately, of course, it would only be someone who had come to see Hazel about a ceremony and hadn't noticed that her pickup wasn't outside. But I was shocked by the sudden noise and hesitated.

The screen opened and George Wanbli came in, his bulldozer belly preceding him, moving everyone and everything in his path aside. I knew he hated Hazel, saw the squint eyed, purse mouthed looks he gave her in public, and I knew he didn't like me either, just because I was Hazel's relative. He frightened me, but now he stood stock still in the middle of the worn linoleum in Hazel's kitchen staring at me as if he was seeing a spirit. I knew then that he hadn't expected anyone to be home, and the banging on the screen door was only a precaution, that I hadn't heard a car drive up in the yard because he hadn't wanted it to be heard. He had probably parked in the shelter belt of trees out by the road, watched Hazel's pickup drive off and then walked to the house.

"What do you want?" I squeaked out, holding the latest almanac behind me, the others scattered, as if George Wanbli would know or even care that I wasn't supposed to mess with them.

In his left hand, he clutched a bundle that looked like feathers and leaves, grayish scraggly herbs that I did not recognize. When he saw my eyes go to it, he thrust it behind his back, and there we stood; each of us hiding something from the other, each of us afraid the other would see what we had. It was an Indian standoff.

He didn't answer my question but replied with one of his own.

"Where's Hazel?"

"Went to town," I said, and then I repeated, "What do you want?"

His eyes left my face, wandered the room, paused hungrily at the cartons in the corner, the cans of coffee and cases of pop stacked on top of other closed boxes, moved on to the iron skillets still sitting on the stove after being heated to dry them and prevent rust, and came back to rest briefly on my face.

"Ummm, I, I . . . ," he stuttered. Caught, he knew, in an act he couldn't explain, but then he seemed to realize that I was only a child, a kid whose only defense was to tell about it later. He cleared his throat then, stood as tall as his big belly would allow, and spoke with that deep voice he used when he wanted to seem authoritative or when he wanted to bully someone into doing something against their better judgment.

"I came to see Hazel about a professional consultation," he said.

I didn't plan to seem pert or challenging, no, indeed, that deep voice of his did frighten me, but the words came out like that anyway.

I said, "And this consultation. It would be about?"

I saw his face darken in the bright sunlit room, his brow lower, and I was not unmindful of his reputation for putting bad spells on people for money, but his own guilt over whatever it was he had planned to do mollified him, even in the face of a challenge from a kid.

"That is a confidential matter," he said.

I didn't know what else to say, but he shuffled his polished black boots on the floor, then looked at his feet as if they had moved on their own volition and took a heavy step backward.

"Tell Hazel I was here," he said as he turned toward the door.

"Oh, I will," I said, braver now that he was leaving. "I sure will tell her."

He didn't look back, but opened the screen door and fled. I wished we had a dog to have warned me of his coming. We used to have one, known by the unimaginative name of Spot, but he had died a year before, and Hazel, with her emotional entanglements tied up in death and loss, would not have another.

I rushed to the window and saw him hot-footing it back down the lane.

Quickly, I gathered up the almanacs, smoothed the bent cover of the one, restacked them, and replaced them on top of the cupboard. What *had* he wanted? What had he come here for, knowing, I was sure, that Hazel was not home and not expecting me to be here either? That bundle in his hands was probably some spell he wanted to put on us, planting the bundle in a place we wouldn't look or wouldn't even know we should look. It would be a curse on us, a curse to ruin Hazel's ceremonies or to make us sick or something—something bad that I couldn't name.

I paced the house, listening for the sound of Hazel's pickup coming home or the sound of another car coming to see Hazel, someone I might know who would make me feel comfortable and safe until Hazel did return. And while I paced, I remembered stories about George Wanbli.

One time George had gotten into an argument with a neighbor, Pete Broussard, who George said had built a barn too close to George's house, maybe even over onto the edge of George's property line, and George had told Pete to move it. Pete had gotten the BIA involved, and when they decided in Pete's favor, George was furious. He told Pete that the place where the barn stood was land possessed of snake spirits who would seek revenge. Pete laughed at him, but then Pete started finding snakes around his house, at first a harmless garden snake curled under his kitchen table and then a big bull snake on his front step. Pete began to think he heard hissing sounds just at the moment he was going to sleep or just as he woke up, hisses that seemed to speak, but in words he couldn't understand. Pete's daughter came to his house after she hadn't seen him for a few days, and there was Pete lying in his bed, swollen up black and green with a dead rattlesnake wrapped around his neck. Some said it was all just coincidence, that snakes were bad that year because it was hot and dry, that they came into houses seeking shade and water, but most people were convinced that George Wanbli had put a spell on Pete. You'd think that fear would have hurt his business as a medicine man, that people would be afraid of him and stay away, but no. It was a demonstration of power, and power could be used to help them with their problems, provided they gave George a big enough gift. Better to have such powerful medicine on your side, they said, but they walked softly and spoke respectfully around him.

By the time Hazel came home I had worked myself into a state, convinced myself that the bundle was snake medicine and that they were already popping into reality under the bed, in the cupboards, and every other place in our cluttered old house. I took a chair outside under the big cottonwood tree at the end of the garden and sat there, but only for a few minutes before I grew afraid that there might be snakes in the tree, waiting to drop down on me and strangle me until I turned black and green like Pete Broussard. When Hazel's pickup clattered up the lane and stopped by the cow shed to unload sacks of feed, I was sitting in the middle of the yard, feet pulled up onto the chair seat, chickens pecking around me and cats looking at me as if I were crazy. I think I was.

I ran to her and grabbed her as if she were the only dry land in a vast ocean, grasped her around the waist and sobbed out the tears I had been afraid to shed. She was a tall woman, big boned and strong, but the force of my run and grasp knocked her back against the pickup door.

"Here! Here!" she said, her arms coming around me. "What could be so awful? What happened?"

The story of George Wanbli's unexpected visit came out in bits between gasps and sobs and snot.

"That old son of a bitch!" Hazel cursed as she put me aside and strode to the house. I thought the old screen door would come off its hinges, she yanked it open so hard. I followed her, reluctantly, not at all sure that Hazel could counter whatever spell George might have put on us, on the house.

I peered through the door at Hazel, standing in the kitchen, her arms folded and one hand holding her chin in thought.

"Watch out for snakes!" I yelled at her.

She looked at me and laughed.

"Snakes. Don't believe everything that people say," she said. "Pete Broussard died of a heart attack."

"But there was a snake around his neck," I protested.

"So some people say," she answered. "Probably just a filthy corner of the sheet that he got tangled around himself while he was dying. He never was too clean in his personal habits."

She walked slowly around the room, touching things lightly, looking carefully at everything.

"But you do ceremonies and spells," I said. "How do you know George Wanbli doesn't? How do you know he doesn't do bad spells on people?"

She came to the door, pulled me gently through, tipping my chin up to look me in the eyes.

"Spirits are real, good and bad," she said. "There are real ceremonies, good and bad, and some people can influence—things. People. Events. But there are people who claim to perform medicine who can't. They use tricks and spread lies to make themselves bigger, to gain advantage. Learn to look with a seeing eye. Learn not to believe every little word that floats in the air."

She sat me down at the table then and put on the tea kettle and didn't say anything until she sat beside me, cups of steaming tea in front of us, tea that we would not usually drink in the warm summer, but perhaps she knew would bring me comfort.

"George Wanbli and people like him are just big old windbags," she said. "If you hadn't been here, he probably would have left that ugly bundle right out on the table. Trying to scare us. And then he would have stolen the money from the jar in the cupboard, and whatever else could stick to his fingers. If you let the air out of a windbag, all you have left is an old empty sack."

"Is the money still there?" I asked.

She took a sip of her tea.

"Did you see him take anything?" she asked.

I shook my head.

"Then how could he have taken it? He isn't a magical being that can do things in front of your eyes that you can't see."

I looked down at my tea, at the leaf flakes floating in the bottom, and didn't answer.

Hazel got up and fetched the money jar from the cupboard, dumped out the bills and the change on the table, and counted it out.

"Ninety-six dollars and eighteen cents," she said. "We had over a hundred and fifty in there, but I took out some to buy chicken feed. He didn't take any."

That simple fact, that reality, comforted me more than her words.

"George Wanbli is an asshole," I said.

"Yes," Hazel responded. "But it's not nice to say 'asshole.'"

"You called him a son of a bitch," I said.

"Yes, I did. And he is."

In spite of Hazel's assurances, after I was in bed, she lit sage and sweetgrass and smudged the house. I saw her come into our bedroom, her face dimly lit by the glowing herbs, smelled the sharp scent and heard her invoking the spirits to cleanse and protect our house.

On May 26, I must have made at least a dozen surreptitious trips to the turkey's nest where she sat calmly and patiently, her beady eyes staring at me as if wondering why I had my nose in her business. There was no chick. There was no chick the next day, nor the next, but still the turkey sat. As the next day passed with no baby turkey hatched, I began to believe in Hazel's insistence that the turkey was only a turkey, a dumb bird fit to grace a dinner table, and not something special or holy. I began to think that I had been wrong about what I thought of as the first miracle, when I believed I had locked the turkey in the hen house, unable to escape, and then it had appeared on the fence in the moonlight later, without ever having had to pass through the closed and pinned door. I wondered if there was some way out of the hen house, a hole under the wall behind the roost, maybe, but I was reluctant to go look for another way out. I wanted to believe in something special, something supernatural beyond Hazel's medicine, but if such did exist against Hazel's insistence, then I might also have to believe in the possible power of George Wanbli. I didn't want to acknowledge that, didn't want nightmares of snakes in my bed, let alone the possible reality of such or something even worse that I couldn't name.

But as each day passed with no turkey chicks hatched, my hopes grew dimmer. Hazel must be right, and that was both disappointing because of the turkey but reassuring because I knew that if the turkey was not holy and special, then neither was George Wanbli, and I could sleep without fear.

On May 29, while the turkey was off her nest eating breakfast with the hens and the black rooster, I took a pan out to her nest and collected the eggs. I carried them out to the cow pen, stood off fifty feet or so from the square corner post, pitched the first egg, and missed the post. The egg went bouncing and rolling off and came to rest in a pile of cow manure. I fished it out with a long, stiff weed, wiping off the worst of the mess on a bunch of grass, and went back to my mark, started to pitch the egg again, and then, for luck, put it aside and picked up another.

It smashed with a satisfying splat followed by that unmistakable stink. How could I have ever thought the turkey was sacred? It was a turkey; it laid eggs that did not turn into chicks, but only rotted and stank like ordinary unfertilized hen eggs. I pitched another egg and watched the greenish slime run down the post. When I had smashed four of the nine, I reached for the first egg, the one that had missed, and hurled it. It hit the post, but did not break. Sometimes that happened. Hazel said it had something to do with the pressure of rotting gas inside the egg. I walked over and picked it up, this time without having to fish it out of a cow pie. It had landed on soft dirt churned up by the cow's hoofs.

The egg quivered in my hand, and I dropped it again. When it fell, a tiny crack appeared across one end, but no slime or stink came out. I knelt beside the egg, and as I watched, another crack appeared. The egg rocked gently in the dirt, and a minute later, another crack opened and a piece of shell fell off, revealing something that looked to me like a patch of wet fur. I picked up the egg and gently peeled off bits of shell until a gawky wet chick sat on the remaining piece of shell in my hand, peeped gently, and almost fell.

I knew then the awe that the Latelys had felt when the turkey had appeared on the fence in the moonlight. I didn't know the Hail Mary, but I had heard prayers in Lakota, wished I had paid more attention to the words, but all I remembered was that it began with *Tunkasila, wakan tanka*. Before I could even utter those words, I heard light running sounds behind me, and turned as the turkey hit me in the face, her wings beating at my head, her spurs scratching my upflung forearms.

I backed away, kicking at her with my feet. *Holy Mary, mother of God.*

She let out a sound then, a turkey sound for sure that had no human translation, and paced back and forth between the pan of eggs sitting on the ground and the floundering chick in front of me.

I sat there and cried, not for the sting of the bloody scratches on my arms, or the fright I had gotten, but because I had been right.

Over the next week, all of the remaining eggs hatched out, and the turkey proudly led her five chicks around the yard, clucking to them and bragging to the chickens about her beautiful babies, babies that would soon lose their baby feathers. Three would be white ones; two would be the brownish, blackish colors of traditional feathers, except that it always seemed to me that the feathers of those two had a dark cast, like the feathers of the black rooster with whom the white mother turkey shared a roost.

3 Stella

Hazel was surprised but not awed by the turkey chicks as I was. She narrowed her eyes, put her hand beneath her chin, one finger across her mouth and eyed them speculatively.

"Dinners," she said. "More dinners. And maybe—if we have both hens and toms—more turkeys."

"But where did they come from?" I asked, still convinced that they were special, not to be eaten, but what else we were to do with them, I had no ideas. The notion of worshiping them as the Latelys had seemed to do struck me as ludicrous, embarrassing. I was not about to kneel in bird poop, did not believe that any spirits would demand such behavior.

"You need to remember the things you are taught," Hazel said.

I knew she meant what she had told me before, that eggs could stay inside the turkey, not growing, but waiting and resting until the turkey had enough food for the egg to mature and be laid. I knew that if a regular egg could do that, so could a fertilized egg, and that the chicks had come from fertilized eggs while the rotten ones had been unfertilized. But how long could a fertilized egg exist inside the turkey? How long from the time a tom turkey mounted the hen until the fertilized egg got laid? Wouldn't there have been too much time between that fertilization and the laying of the eggs by our hen? How much time would it take? My brain couldn't wrap itself around those notions of time and perhaps and maybes and certainties, but there was no mystery in Hazel's mind: the hen had mated with a tom turkey, escaped the slaughter house, run, and arrived on our doorstep and laid the eggs that hatched into our chicks. The exact details of the turkey's arrival were unknown to us, but she believed that there was a factual series of events, logically explainable. While I wondered and marveled, Hazel had other work to do, other events that occupied her thoughts.

I always knew that Hazel owned our place, that it was her father's original allotment, 160 acres with the house, the tin cow shed, the chicken coop, the pens, even the old barn that we'd been too poor to keep in good repair until finally a big wind had blown it down two years ago. All that and the garden took up only a couple of acres. The rest of the land, except for the twenty acres of pasture for the cow, was good farmland but impossible for us to plant, tend, harvest. Hazel hadn't the money or the credit to buy the equipment that farming would take, so she leased the land out, had done so for years to a white farmer named Jack Olsen.

Because of the Bureau of Indian Affairs rules stuck on Indian owners, Olsen couldn't pay his leasing fees directly to Hazel but instead had to pay the money through the leasing officer of the tribe, where that office recorded all the payments and then passed them on to the landowners in twice-a-year payments. George Wanbli held the job of tribal leasing officer, but he was never in the office. He turned the job over mostly to his minion, Johnson Powers, while George continued as a practicing medicine man. How could he get away with that, some people might ask, and the answer was because his cousin, Elias Villiers, was tribal council chair with the ability to appoint relatives to plum jobs and not fire them for not showing up and turning the work itself over to subordinates.

Indian landowners had to go to the tribal leasing office twice a year, in January and July, to collect their payments in person. I liked it that way because Hazel never made me stand in line with her but let me run around outside with my friends. Hazel liked collecting her checks in person, too, I think, for the same reasons. It's good to see friends, whether you're a kid or an adult. But in March, Hazel had gotten a letter that made her clamp her mouth down in the way she does when she is very unhappy with someone, but this time I knew it wasn't me. She said it was nothing important, just that the leasing office had sent notice that they would be mailing the checks in the future, so no one would have to come in to pick them up. It wasn't only that she liked seeing her friends, she said, but she didn't want to give Johnson Powers, the deputy leasing officer, any opportunity to say "the check's in the mail." She didn't trust him. The next day she sent a letter telling him she would pick up her checks as usual. Two weeks later, she got another letter saying that everyone would have their check mailed; they could not make an exception for her. Hazel sent another letter. Powers replied.

So, now the letter war had gone on for two months, until finally Hazel had sent a registered letter, not to Johnson Powers, but to his boss, the senior leasing officer himself, George Wanbli.

"If I didn't know better, I'd think George is doing this to me for some ulterior reason," she said, "but I can't believe that he would go to the trouble of punishing every other Indian land owner just to get at me." She fretted about it, but she had other things to keep her busy, and I just did the chores and stayed out of her way.

Sun Dance was coming up, the most sacred event of the cycle of ceremonies for the year, and as a medicine woman, Hazel helped some of the participants to prepare both spiritually and physically. In one way, they had been preparing for the entire previous year, saving their money to buy perishable goods just before the ceremony and making items to be contributed to the giveaway that accompanied the ceremony. The giveaway was an obligation felt by most participants, a thanks offering to the spirits for their intentions, whether that was something they begged of the spirits for the future, or something good that had happened in the past for which they felt grateful. The made items were sometimes traditional, sometimes not—beaded tobacco pouches, knife sheaths, moccasins, ribbon shirts as were made in the distant past for such events, and modern items like ladies' purses and sewn canvas backpacks, as well as items that mixed old traditions and new needs, like beaded watch bands. Just before the giveaway, the Sun Dance participant would take the money that they had saved along with any donations from friends and relatives and go on a shopping trip to Rapid City where they would buy sweatshirts, towels and sheets, and perishable items such as cans of coffee and cases of soda pop. All of this wasn't directly given to the spirits, of course, but to people who attended the Sun Dance.

That was the practical aspect of preparation, in which Hazel held no part. The sacred part, the purification part, that was her concern. Participants were to go to the ceremony with a good heart—*cante waste*—and for each dancer, that meant retreat from the world for a week or a few days prior to contemplate the purpose for participation—prayer, lots of prayer, and an *inipi*, a sweat lodge ceremony right before the Sun Dance itself. During the week before, Hazel was gone much of the time, going from house to house of her dancers, encouraging them quietly, praying with them.

The day before the dance was to begin, all five of Hazel's dancers came to our place for the *inipi*. In the days of my childhood, women might dance at the official ceremony to encourage the participants, but the special part of the ceremony, the ultimate level of participation, was the piercing, and that was exclusively a man's province. It went back, way back to traditional times. A man would be purified by retreat into contemplation and prayer, followed by a sweat lodge ceremony, and then at the Sun Dance, the medicine man would pierce his chest muscles in two places, insert sticks in the wounds connected by leather thongs and tied by a much longer thong to the Sun Dance tree in the center. Then the dancer circled the pole, staring at the sun and praying while pulling back against the thong until the sticks broke through the flesh. That sounds gory and painful and masochistic to your average Christian, but to us, the notion of the Christian communion is even worse—that the bread and wine are supposed to turn into the body and blood of Christ—transubstantiation—horrified us even more. We might sacrifice our own flesh, endure pain for a cause, but we never engaged in cannibalism.

George Wanbli always had ten or more acolytes who participated in the piercing at the Sun Dance, but Hazel abhorred his methods. She believed that the preceding sweat ceremony should be meaningful; George turned it into an endurance contest without meaning. He heated the rocks that were put into the lodge too hot, poured too much water on them and created too much steam, made it so hot that lungs burned and people fainted. George declared that anyone who left the lodge too early because of major discomfort was unfit to proceed with the Sun Dance. George considered fainting and having to be pulled out by the feet as a sign of strength and a good heart. Hazel said that anyone who went that far went too far.

George also pierced too deep, as if he believed that only a sacrifice of great pain would be meaningful, and the knife he used wasn't clean to start with and wasn't cleaned between piercings of individuals, so many of his dancers sickened afterward. One of them had died of blood poisoning, an event that George passed off by saying that the man's intentions had not been pure, that he had not approached the ceremony with a good heart, that he had polluted the ceremony and the spirits had retaliated. You'd think that death would have made other future participants avoid George and seek the assistance of other medicine men, but no, people seemed to think that George's failure only proved his superiority and competence.

"Some people are fools," Hazel said, "and should be avoided."

I wondered who were the fools, George or the participants who went to him.

Some years, Hazel had no participants to prepare for the Sun Dance, but most years, she had one or two. This year there were five, four men and one woman. We both knew that the appearance of the white turkey at Hazel's place had brought more people seeking her assistance for the Sun Dance, just as it had brought more people in general asking for her services.

"It's not like I had a visitation from White Buffalo Woman," she grumbled. But she knew that practically, what people believed about the white turkey had brought her more people.

"Well, if you throw enough shit against the wall, sooner or later some of it will stick. Or someone will see a picture of the Virgin Mary in it," she said.

The gossipers had spread enough around about Hazel's unwillingness to talk about the sacredness of the white turkey so that people knew better than to mention anything about it when they came to the house, and the Sun Dancers who came for the *inipi* ceremony at our house were no exception, though they stared and looked nervous when they saw the turkey with her chicks pecking at odd bits of stones and chasing grasshoppers.

We were to camp out at the Sun Dance like almost everyone else, not even going home to do chores and feed the animals. Our near neighbors, a pair of aging bachelor brothers, Albert and Ansel Kiefer, did that for us every year, and we reciprocated at christmas when they went to Chicago to visit their family.

On the opening day of the ceremony, cars crowded each other parked willy-nilly in the pasture near the creek where the ceremony was to be held up in Yellow Bear Canyon. It was supposed to be a closed ceremony, only Lakota people, a tradition that harked back to the days when it was banned by the Indian agents, and people were punished for attending, but always word got out, and that year was no different. Crowds of white tourists came, bringing their L.L. Bean camping gear, their coolers of food and beer, barbecue grills, lawn chairs, and roving packs of screaming kids that ran through the camp. And their cameras. Those are strictly forbidden, but what are you going to do? Set up a perimeter fence and checkpoints with armed guards? In those days, people felt that you couldn't enforce respect, only ask for it.

We had an army surplus tent that Hazel shooed me out of so she could advise the dancers that she was sponsoring. I didn't mind because it gave me a chance to find my friends, especially Avril. He had stopped asking me about the white turkey.

We roamed the grounds dodging in and out among the tents pitched at random, usually family groups camping together and in that way, it was not unlike the old days when family groups traveled together and set up their tipis near each other for companionship and sharing of labor and whatever else one group had that the other didn't. Smoke from campfires drifted over the tents, smells of roasting meat and bubbling coffee pots, sounds of conversation and muted—usually muted—laughter. It was after all, a religious occasion, the most solemn and sacred event of the year. Hazel had already warned me repeatedly about acting like the wild white kids. Avril and I stopped here and there to talk to kids we knew, avoiding the parents and older people who would find some chores for us to do.

In midsummer, the sun doesn't go down until near nine o'clock or after, but I knew when it got dark, I had to be back at the tent before Hazel came looking for me with a switch. The Sun Dance would begin at sunrise, and that came early.

In keeping with the notion of contemplation, the tents and camper trailers of those who would participate in the ceremony were all off to one side from the main group, pitched or parked close to their sponsors, the medicine men, or women as in Hazel's case. Avril stopped at his family's camper, and I hurried on to our tent in the growing dusk, trying to avoid tripping over hummocks of grass in the twilight. I was late, so I took a shortcut through the camp circle of George Wanbli, taking advantage of the light streaming from a window in his camper to see where I was going. It was an old camper, the kind with the windows in narrow overlapping panels that fold out and up when you turn a crank, and the light fell in bars on the ground. As I was about to step into the light, I heard Hazel's name uttered with something akin to contempt, a low guttural sound as if the name were spat out like a rotten cherry, an insult that hit me and stopped me right outside that open window.

Inside, a man and a woman argued in low, intense voices, George Wanbli, I knew, and probably his wife, Dorothy, a woman almost as big as George but always retiring and quiet, at least in his presence. I had no idea that she would stand up to him in private, but her voice coming through the window was firm and steady.

"It's just wrong," she said. "You'll bring it back on yourself. And you risk others, too. Benny, Joe—you're supposed to be their guide, but you're using them in a bad way."

"Benny and Joe volunteered, so it's on them, not me. They know I can do everything I promise and more. They want what I can give them, and besides, you act like everything is going to go wrong. Have you no faith in me? In my medicine?"

"George, everyone knows you have strong medicine. But so does Hazel Latour."

"In a head-to-head matchup, if there was such a thing, I'd win every time. But she doesn't even know what's going on, so how could she do anything about it anyway?" He paused a moment, and then he said, in a rising vicious tone, "I'll bury her. I'll bury her so deep not even a badger could dig her up."

"Shhh," Dorothy said. "Such things should not even be whispered. They might hear."

"Who? Who? There's no one around. Here, I'll prove it."

There was the sound of heavy footsteps, and I jerked back against the shadow of the camper as the camper door was flung open, George partially appeared and then abruptly jerked back inside. A mosquito hummed beside my ear.

"George! Not people, I'm not talking about people. Spirits! The spirits will hear."

"Don't put your hands on me, woman," George growled.

"All right. All right." Dorothy's voice was almost inaudible above the mosquito. "But it's on you, not me."

George's laughter barked sharply.

"I'm not afraid of Hazel Latour or any spirits she can call up," he said, and then I heard footsteps, someone walking close. I dropped down and rolled under the low camper, banging my head loudly on the steel frame and uttering a groan that seemed as loud as thunder to me, surely loud enough to bring George with his big fists, or worse yet, his charms and curses, but at the same time, someone pounded loudly on the door of George's camper, masking my sounds. From beneath the camper, I saw feet, big feet in lace-up hunting boots.

"WHAT?" George said as he jerked open the camper door and a shaft of light illuminated the boots.

"I came for the final prayers," the man's voice said.

"Joe," George said, somewhat milder. "Where's Benny?"

"He'll be along in a few minutes. He was tanking up on food knowing we can't eat or drink anything for three days. I think he ate too much or something didn't agree with him. If he doesn't stop shitting before tomorrow, he'll be a pretty sight in the Sun Dance." He made a wheezing sound that I supposed was laughter, stepped up into the camper, and closed the door.

I didn't hear if Dorothy or George made an answer. I rolled out from under the camper and ran, but I was looking back over my shoulder, caught a foot on the guyline of someone's tent opposite George's trailer, and laid myself out full length on the hard, hummocky ground. I had scraped my shin on the rope, banged my knees, and in catching my foot, had given a jerk to the tent that had aroused someone inside. I heard a half-asleep mumbling through the tent wall, and saw the muted glow of a flashlight beam. I got up and ran stumbling for Hazel's tent, shin and knees stinging, head throbbing from the thump on the steel undercarriage of George's camper, holding back sobs, and feeling warm and wet on my legs. I had peed my pants.

I was panting when I flung myself through the tent flaps and almost on top of Hazel on her knees rolling out the sleeping bags.

"Where have you been?" she said sternly, but I couldn't answer immediately, only sank panting onto the half-unrolled camouflage colored sleeping bag, another army surplus purchase that felt soft and comforting now.

"What have you been up to that you had to run from?" Hazel demanded.

I shook my head, got up and pumped a cup of water from the jug on the stool by the open tent flap, conscious of the wet vee on the inside of my pants legs, front and back.

"I'm sorry I'm late," I said, "but . . ."

"With you, my dear, there is always a 'but,' isn't there? What is it this time?" But then her eyes shifted from the sleeping bags to look directly at me, from my disheveled hair and teary face to the dirt on my hands and arms and my wet pants.

"*Takoja.*" The word came softly from her lips, a word that she used so rarely I had almost forgotten its meaning. Grandchild.

Hazel was disturbed, had seen that my condition was not just the result of a fall in the dark or a disagreement with a friend, but something deeper and serious.

Her hesitation lasted only a minute, and then she was standing, pouring water into a basin, rummaging in a bag and bringing out clean underwear, a clean shirt to sleep in and talking all the time, in that fast, low way that she did when she was thinking, ordering her thoughts beneath her talk and distracting me from my panic, from the humiliation of having wet my pants like a baby.

In a moment she had the clothes laid out on a sleeping bag, had stripped my clothes off and sat me on a folding camp cot. She dipped a washcloth, wrung it out, and pushing my hair off my face began gently sponging off the dirt and tears.

I started to speak, but my chest felt choked and full, my throat closed with tears. She put the washcloth against my lips.

"Shhh. In a few minutes, you will tell me everything. But now, you will just sit, close your eyes, and think about tulips."

Oh. Tulips. Every year in January the seed catalogue came in the mail, bringing hope that spring *would* come, that the deep, seemingly endless cold and snow would go away, that there would be warm rain, mating coyotes howling in the distance and very straight rows of quarter-inch-high green sprouts of carrot and radishes in Hazel's garden, located close to the well so it wouldn't be so far to carry water during the times the rain did not come often enough or hard enough. I loved those color pictures in that seed catalog, the orange pumpkins big as a house, it seemed, the red tomatoes in a dozen or more varieties, the green of cucumbers, and the pictures of watermelons, so perfect that while the wind howled outside, I could smell them, could taste their sweet nectar and even feel the stickiness of juice on my hands and see the hard black seeds that I loved to spit at the cats. But as much as Hazel and I loved all the vegetable descriptions, loved reading the descriptions beside each picture (*fifty-five days to maturity, plant after all danger of frost is past, keep evenly watered*), we both loved the flowers the best, especially the tulips. I don't know why we preferred tulips. Maybe it was their form, elegantly simple, without a pretentious frothiness of petals, or the rich colors of the classic tulips contrasted against the deep green, long squashed heart shape of the leaves, in pairs on each side of the thick central stem, or the silky feel of the petals. Probably all of this.

If we had been wealthy or evenly moderately well off, we would have spent more money decorating the outside than the inside of whatever house we had, but when Hazel and I dream shopped, neither of us had much enthusiasm for planning houses. It was always the flowers, and always the tulips above all.

In most places, tulips bloom for two springs, sometimes for three, but in South Dakota one is more usual, so every year we ordered half a dozen tulip bulbs, all we could really afford. In lucky years when the previous year's bulbs had been particularly hardy, we might have as many as ten bulbs blooming simultaneously in the bed on the warmer south side of the house, right up tight against the foundation and covered over with chicken wire to keep those pesky birds from getting at them.

We debated, the two of us, over which ones to buy, usually what color. A few times we had ordered all one color, usually our favorite red. Once or twice when money was tighter than ever, we ordered the grab-bag special, and got whatever colors they had, sometimes mixed, but one year it was a deep dark purple, still beautiful but our least favorite color. We didn't want something dark, oh no, but something bright and happy that would put the first of a pair of parentheses around the warmer season of the year. The second parenthesis, the closing one, well, that is another story for another time.

The year before we had chosen three red and three soft pink, planted them in the fall, and pushed them to the back of our minds until the seed catalog came in January, reminding us that there would be tulips in a few weeks. Even though this year had seen the coming of the turkey, that had not taken any joy from the tulip blooming.

I saw them in my mind, their perfect shape, about ten inches tall, waving slightly in the cool spring breeze, remnants of old snow-banks still hiding in shady spots. This year there had been no sur-vivors from the previous year's planting, but that did not signify; we never counted on it, and when it happened it was a bonus.

Hazel and I had stooped in front of the bed and gently stroked the silky petals and told each other they were soft as a kitten, soft as a newly hatched chick, slightly shiny, almost luminescent, and we thought up comparisons for the color. That red ones had turned out slightly orange, like the sunset on a dusty, windy day, and the pink one reminded us of the tiny pink hearts of navy beans, cooked until some of the hearts came away and floated on the surface of the soup. Yes. Tulips are pure expressions of undiluted joy.

"Stand up."

I opened my eyes. Hazel was kneeling with a soft towel. I stepped into it and was enveloped in the towel and Hazel's hug.

"Better?" she asked, and I was.

She started to help me dress, but I pulled away and dressed myself. I had to maintain some dignity.

And while I sat on my sleeping bag in my clean but softly worn old shirt, Hazel smoothed an ointment on my barked shin and combed my hair.

I told her what I had overheard, adding, "I'm afraid of them."

She put down the comb and hugged me again.

"You are safe here with me. No one is going to harm you."

"I don't mean now," I said. "George Wanbli is planning to do something bad to you. I don't know what."

She turned me to face her and looked directly into my eyes.

"George Wanbli isn't nearly as powerful as he thinks he is," she said. "I can take care of myself. Don't you have any confidence in me?"

I looked away.

"Yes, but . . ."

"But what?"

"But he is getting Benny and Joe to help him do something."

Hazel laughed.

"Benny and Joe. Joe and Benny. Who are they? Just think about it for a bit, little one. Who are the two people always getting arrested for being drunk and disorderly? Who are the two people whose own families are embarrassed by them? Are they really any kind of threat?"

"Not really, but how come they are in the Sun Dance, then? I thought you couldn't be in it if you were a bad person."

"That's the way it's supposed to be, but who can look into someone else's heart and tell if they're participating for the right reasons or not? I don't want that job. And maybe, maybe, they are trying to reform themselves. So, if they're trying to reform themselves, that's a good thing and means you shouldn't worry. And if they are bad people doing bad things, remember what fools they are and don't think they can do bad things and get away with it."

I nodded reluctantly without saying aloud that I felt something else about those two, that with direction and encouragement, even fools could be dangerous. I suspected Hazel knew that, too, but was pretending otherwise to comfort me.

"Go to sleep. We have to get up before sunrise tomorrow," she said.

I lay down on my sleeping bag, the evening too warm to cover up, but I knew that by morning, the air would be very cool, and I would be glad to be inside the bag. As sleep crept upon me, I smiled. Hazel had not mentioned that I had wet my pants.

4 Hazel

I had called her *takoja*, a word that I kept walled off from my thoughts and rarely, rarely let slip past my lips. She is all I have left of her mother, this precious one, and I am so afraid that if certain spirits see how beloved she is to me, they will take her, too, for what purpose, for what I have done, I cannot know, for I am not perfect, but I have never deliberately harmed anyone.

It was not the sight of her terrified staring eyes, or the torn knees of her jeans, the tangled mess of her hair that elicited that word I usually repressed. I had seen her in worse condition, when she fell after being chased halfway across the pasture by an angry badger, for instance. No, that was not it. It was the sight of that dark wetness on the inside of her jeans smelling of ammonia. She had been the easiest child in the world to potty train because she hated the feel of anything wet or nasty against her bottom. When she was two years old she had come in off the front porch crying with embarrassment, her tiny corduroy pants wet, and said, "I didn't mean to! I didn't mean to! I was just playing and the pee jumped out." I remember laughing and then stifling it when she buried her head on my shoulder, sobbed harder, and would not look at me.

For her to wet her pants meant something had terrified her beyond the moment, so deeply that her bladder, so controlled, had let go.

Takoja. I said it once more in my head, to fix that sound so when I could no longer bring myself to utter it, even silently, the memory, the feeling of what the word meant, could still be recalled.

I reached my arm out and touched her, breathing softly, deep asleep. I hoped that I had planted the image of tulips so strongly that she would dream of them, beautiful glorious fields of them, and not be disturbed with nightmares of evil men, evil plans, and evil deeds.

I had not been honest with her, which I believe she knew, but sometimes the pretense of serenity is almost as good as the truth of it. George Wanbli was a jealous man, vindictive and cruel, and his own poor wife had often publicly borne the evidence of George's fists, trying to keep her head up and pretend that same serenity that I had tried to project tonight. Why is it that the women are the ones who must be the peacemakers, the pourers of oil on troubled waters?

I knew George well, and I also knew that this time there was more going on than just George's professional jealousy that some of his followers had deserted his spiritual practices for mine. He had another plan afoot, something, if I did not mistake, that meant more to him than his reputation, which had in any case become more than a bit diminished and ragged around the edges over the past five years or so. But what was at the bottom of George's malice? Where did his motive lie?

I sketched a brief biography of him in my head, thinking that might lead me to a supposition at least, an idea. I needed to figure it out, to forestall whatever he might be planning for whatever reason.

George was older than me by six years. He, too, had been sent to boarding school at Marty Mission, but as I was an only child, my parents had held me out of school an extra year, reluctant to part with me, and George had dropped out of school after the seventh grade, leaving the year before I began, so I did not have the pleasure of knowing him until a few years later, when I was in my early teens and home for the summer. I had heard of his antics many times, but the first time I actually saw him, he was walking about the rides of the carnival that had set up that year in conjunction with the pow-wow at Ghost Hawk Canyon over on Rosebud. He was with a group of young men about his age, early twenties, I suppose, and drinking. George was always bigger than the people he ran with, probably deliberately chose friends smaller than him so he could feel physically superior, could use his size to bully them into agreeing with him. At this pow-wow, he had put his money down at one of those side shows where you test your strength by hitting a pad with a big hammer that sends a marker up a pole: where it stopped, well, that indicated what prize you got, and George was not happy with his prize, a red pressed-glass vase. I remember him yelling at the carnival worker, who would not give him his money back or let George try again. George had picked up the vase and smashed it on the counter and used a sharp piece of glass to slash the carnival worker's face, cutting off half the man's nose, would have taken out an eye, too, if the guy hadn't jumped back, blood gushing between the fingers of his hand that he used trying to hold the piece of his nose on.

That first impression of George as a mean spirited, violent bully had never changed. His actions at the carnival in plain sight of so many people had brought shame on his family, so they took him in hand, insisted that he stop running around and drinking—well, at least not as much as before—and got him a job at the BIA. It wasn't any big deal; he was an assistant to the guy who kept track of leases—Indian land being leased to other Indians sometimes, but mostly to non-Indians. It was a ten-hour-a-week job that without much ingenuity could be stretched into a forty-hour-a-week pretense. And when George's good-time drinking buddies began to drift away, he found another way to gain sycophantic followers. He started studying medicine ways with Leonard Knife, a very old, respected elder. At first it was probably idle curiosity, maybe even another condition mandated by his family, but one year, George had assisted Leonard at ceremonies with a bored look on his face and barely suppressed yawns, and the next year the yawns and boredom had gone, replaced with an alert look that most people mistook for intensity and even spiritual blessedness, but my own father believed that look was deviousness, alternative motives underneath, and while my father was not a man to speak ill of people, he mentioned it once after a *hunka* ceremony, to my mother and me. After that, I noticed too, and I believed I saw what my father had seen.

George had married Dorothy when they were both older. Dorothy had planned to be a nun but had lost her vocation along with her virginity, some said. Others said she had been raped by George, who tricked her into an abortion with one of his herbal concoctions, and that her parents had insisted that he marry her, baby or no. There had been no children born of the marriage.

George still worked for the BIA leasing department, but now he headed it, and instead of stretching ten hours of work a week into forty, he now did no work at all but had four assistants, each stretching ten hours of work a week into forty, while George solicited clients for his medicine man practice out of his office or was absent altogether, probably conducting private ceremonies or praying, most people believed. People talked about George's lazy ways, taking money for work he did not do, but they secretly applauded him, too, because for them, BIA money was government money, not tribal money, and any money an Indian could get out of a government that represented the people who had oppressed them for five hundred years justified the means of getting it. It was the new way of attacking a circle of wagons without killing anyone.

What was he really doing while he was gone from his office? I wondered. Knowing that might tell me what George was really planning to do and why he seemed to think I would be a hindrance to whatever those plans were. There had to be some reason other than just jealousy of my medicine ways practice. If it hadn't been for her—I reached out and touched her cheek in the darkness—I might not now be lying awake worrying over whatever evil he planned to do. But George might think that my little one was also a hindrance to whatever scheme he had planned. I remembered the slashed and bloodied nose of the carnival worker. George might have become more subtle, more circumspect as he had aged, but I did not doubt that he could be just as vicious if he felt threatened.

I needed a plan, I told myself, but before any ideas could present themselves, I drifted off to sleep.

The camp stirred like a sleeping giant in the early dawn. I let Stella sleep, dressing myself in the barely relieved darkness. The Sun Dancers that I was counseling scratched on the tent flap; I raised it and stepped outside. We walked off to the edge of the camp, over a little ridge out of sight, and there we stopped, sat, and I lit my pipe and led them through the final prayers before their ordeal would begin.

Sleepy, murmuring people moved slowly but purposefully in groups and trickles towards the dance ground, children wrapped in blankets carried by adults, old people leaning on the arm of a younger person, drawn like iron filings towards the horse-shoe shaped pavilion, a series of parallel pine poles planted in the ground, topped with cross pieces and covered with the cut branches of pine, softly perfuming the dawn. Then those who would perform the sacred dance came in single file and advanced toward the single pole in the middle, arranging themselves in a semicircle facing the pole and the horizon, waiting for the sun to rise. From the immeasurable vastness of midnight blue, the sky shaded down in delicate violet to light blue just there on the horizon where the first thin golden arc rose. Rays of light shot across the hills like holy water flung from the spirits to bless those who would dance, those who would observe, those who would guide, and even the children, who were too young and innocent to understand but, nevertheless, were present. The presiding medicine man, an elderly man who had been carried to his place beneath the pole, faced the sun, raised his arms, and offered the prayer that would begin the ceremony.

I sat under the pavilion with the other medicine people who were guides for dancers and next to us, the first group of drummers. There were several groups who would take turns throughout the long day, but for the dancers, there would be no reprieve until the sun set, when they would be led to separate tents some distance off from the rest of the camp to rest until the following morning. It would last three days. Spectators could come and go as they pleased, but family and friends of each dancer tried to spend as much time as they could bear at the pavilion, praying for their dancer, encouraging them. It is a holy ceremony, much like an all-day Christian service in the solemnity, the beat of the drums interrupted by the occasional cry of an infant, the rustling of legs trying to get a more comfortable position, the snoring of an old person lulled into sleep. When the drum group changes, many people use that small confusion to take a nature break at the portapotties positioned discreetly behind a few pines close to the pavilion, or to get a drink of water. It is difficult to sit so long, to concentrate on prayer, and I find my mind wanders. I suspect everyone's does; we are, after all, humans only trying to be something higher.

I remembered early morning mass at boarding school, being

harangued out of our hard dormitory beds at sunrise by the youngest nuns, not realizing at the time that someone else, some older nun, probably the sour-faced Sister Bertilla, had likely harangued the young nuns out of bed even earlier. And who awakened Bertilla? In retrospect, I wondered did the woman ever sleep, wondered if she sat up all night thinking up new ways to annoy, to harass, to trouble not only the students, but her sisters, and even the mother superior, who was the only person superior to Bertilla, unless you counted the priest, Father Alfonso. Mostly, he, too, was cowed by Bertilla. He was harmless enough for the students, a little round man with a face that shined with sweat no matter the season, always seeming in a hurry, probably to escape from Bertilla, who constantly bedeviled him about one thing or the other, towering over the little man, trying to persuade him to invoke some new, oppressive rules that she hadn't been able to persuade Mother to agree to.

I remember being numb with sleep, mechanically pulling on clothes, pushed and prodded by the older students who hissed, "Hurry up, do you want punishment?" and the nuns, who probably also worried about a punishment, lining us up in order of height and marching us out into the long hall, down the stairs, and outside where we were joined with another snaking line of equally sleep-benumbed children from the boys' dormitory. Then the short march to the tolling bell of the church, the clumsy student behind sometimes stepping on your heels, the dipping of fingers into the holy water, genuflecting, making the sign of the cross, marching to the pews, genuflecting again, sitting on benches polished and smooth by years of children's behinds, and just as we began to wake up, the soporific chant of the mass began. When I was little, an older student told me that the instances in the mass where you had to move from sitting to standing to kneeling and back again were designed to keep people from going to sleep. As I got older, I laughed at such a notion, but now that I am older still, I am back to believing the student. Belief is like that, a circle, and often I find that the seemingly simplistic explanations from childhood for the unexplainable have merit, maybe more so than all the educated and contrived answers of adulthood.

I retain almost nothing of those early masses. They taught me nothing that I have carried forward with me except for the absolute conviction that all churches are cold for three hundred and sixty days out of the year and hot for five days. I know some of my people who must have gotten something of value from that Christian teaching, people like the Latelys, other individuals and families who took Christian teachings and folded them into the fabric of their lives. Like herb sprigs placed between towels to keep away moths, I suppose, those Christian teachings kept away the evil from their lives, or at least they must believe they do, or why bother at all?

Then there are some people who believe in both Christianity and our traditional beliefs and practices and see no conflict, and some like me who reject Christianity entirely and practice only traditional belief. Maybe not like me, though, because I mix my traditional practice with a healthy—I think—a healthy dose of practicality. I believe the spirits help those who help themselves, to borrow an idea from the Christians. See? Maybe I did retain something of Christianity after all. You can't live your life like a coyote, spending half your life trying to trick others out of what they have instead of working for it yourself and the other half of your life sitting on your butt and howling.

George sat two people away and a little in front me in the pavilion, so I could see his face clearly only when he turned his head to watch the dancers as they moved around the pole. Age had taught him a constraint that had not been there as a youth. His personality was not the type to sit still, but yet here he was, not only sitting quietly but with an involved and interested expression on his face. I wondered how long he had practiced to achieve that semblance of interest and humility. And again, I wondered what plan he had that involved keeping me silenced or at least discrediting me as a medicine person. I did not believe that George would do violence against me. Age had not only taught him to keep his emotions hidden, but also to be sneakier in his actions. As far I knew, he had not hacked anyone's nose off since that years-ago incident, and hadn't beaten up on anyone except Dorothy. He did not need to. His reputation as a strong medicine person has put many in fear of what he could induce evil spirits to do for his benefit. I did not believe he had any power to do such things, but people are gullible, and if you offer them supernatural reasons for unfortunate events brought about by natural causes, they rarely want to believe the common, logical explanations. It is more dramatic, more exciting to believe that they were the target of some malicious spirits set in motion by an enemy.

I am not a fool. I do believe that some people have such abilities to engage spirits in their cause, but what set of spirits would voluntarily assist or even be tricked into assisting someone as stupid and mean-spirited as George Wanbli? It is like UFO sightings. Probably ninety-nine out of a hundred have perfectly natural, albeit odd, explanations, but one in a hundred is *wakan*, unexplainable and far beyond our meager human capacity to understand.

At noon Stella brought me a sandwich, which I ate behind the pavilion as I walked around stretching my legs, thinking. She seemed calmer today, rested and not nervous, because, like me, George had to be here in attendance at the ceremony and nowhere near where she might be. I cautioned her not to eat too much junk food from the food booths over on the opposite side of camp, and not to get overheated running around in the sun with her friends. She rolled her eyes, gave me that look that said, "I'm almost a grown-up, so stop treating me like a child," and walked away.

The afternoon went as these ceremonies usually do, uneventfully, unless you counted the fuss when a couple of little boys got into a punch-up under the pavilions and their fathers had to drag them away. Then there were the white tourists, who meant well, I suppose, and were trying to participate in the ceremony, except that one white woman kept hollering, *"Hoka he!"* It means something like "let's go" or "we are ready now," and I suppose she meant it to encourage the dancers, but she didn't know that Lakota is a gendered language, so to hear this male expression coming from a woman was not an encouragement but an embarrassment. Still, even serious ceremonies can stand some comic relief.

By the afternoon, the dancers looked strong, but then most people could manage the first day. It is the afternoon of the second day that starts to tell on them.

When the sun had set, people went to their campsites to eat their dinners, everything from pots of beans watched and stirred alternatively by those watching the dancers and those taking a break, to hamburgers and hot dogs grilled outside, or Indian tacos purchased from Jonnie Lone Tree's food booth, a refitted camper, or one of the others. I would not eat anything from Jonnie's stand. I had visited her house a couple of times and seen the condition of her kitchen. I was suspicious of the other food vendors, too.

Stella had the charcoal in our little grill going when I arrived at our tent after spending an hour talking and praying with my three dancers. They seemed strong still, and determined. It did not hurt that their families had been very obviously in attendance all day, sitting right in the middle of the pavilion and calling out encouragement.

It is amazing how good simple food tastes when you are hungry. We ate our hot dogs, pork and beans, and pickles off paper plates, sitting by our tent and chatting with people who walked by already done with their supper, and fending off the occasional dog that got too bold. After, we, too, walked around the camp, stopping here and there to visit with family or friends. When you grow up in a small, closed community you know almost everybody, and even those that you do not like very much are part of the whole, like a flaw in a favorite dress that would not have the same value and uniqueness if it were perfect.

When we went to bed I was content with myself except that I still had no idea of what George Wanbli was up to—and until I had some idea, I could make no plan. That was worrisome.

The next day proceeded as the previous one had done, although the fasting and physical exertion had begun to take a toll on the dancers. People with chronic health problems like heart conditions or diabetes are discouraged from participating, but there are always some few who foolishly believe that the spirits will protect them from any harm. There is no vetting process, no medical examiner who says this one can participate, that one cannot. At least a third of the dancers dropped out, unable to force themselves to go on. They left the dance arena with their heads down, embarrassed at their failure, but no one thought less of them. It is arduous, and not everyone makes it through the first attempt. There is always the next year, a whole year to prepare for another try.

On the third and last day right after noon, one of the women dancers, a woman who had no medicine person as a sponsor, turned gray as a winter sky, stumbled, and dropped like a stone. She was lifted up and carried to the shade of the pavilion, but as soon as she roused, she heaved herself up and tried to return to the dance, but her family held her back. I heard whispers to the effect that the woman was diabetic, and the fasting had probably—certainly—upset her blood sugar. Some thought her holy for making such an attempt. I thought her foolish. She probably had no sponsor because those she had approached had told her they would not sponsor someone whose medical condition was not optimal.

George Wanbli had an expression on his face that I could not read, an expression that he quickly suppressed. It seemed like disgust or, more probably, contempt, which would not surprise me, since everyone knew that George pushed his own acolytes beyond reason, turning everything into an endurance contest when, except for the Sun Dance itself, that was not a part of traditional spiritual practice. For George, physical weakness was blasphemy.

Another hour passed while I watched George, who had gotten twitchy and anxious as if he were dancing in the heat instead of sitting in the shade with a bottle of pop at his side. He watched the dancers, glanced at his watch, drummed his fingers on his knee, eased himself from one side to the other. And then I saw Benny come dancing round the pole and glance at George, who seemed to nod, almost imperceptibly.

Benny went down. Instantly, George was on his feet and weaving his way through the other dancers to Benny, leaning over him and feeling his forehead while Benny's brothers and uncles came out to stand and stare. George helped roll Benny onto a blanket and helped carry him into the section of the pavilion where I sat with the other medicine people and the drummers. They laid him down on the side away from me, but I saw Benny's face. He was sweating heavily, drenched even. That's not usual, because by the second day, the dancers have sweated out most of their excess body fluid, and since they are fasting—no food or water—there is little water to sweat out. Third-day dancers have to be watched very carefully. Anyone who stops sweating completely and starts to shiver is on the edge of heatstroke. George had pushed his people to that edge and beyond many times, yet he seemed solicitous of Benny. Something was not right here, but I did not know what and did not think about it much beyond the curiosity level. Whether or not Benny finished his Sun Dance pledge had nothing to do with whatever George was planning for me, or so I thought. Two of my people had dropped out, but the others seemed all right still. I would watch them carefully for the rest of this day and even more so on the next.

The afternoon seemed interminable. If it was so for me, it had to be even more so for the nine dancers still on their feet, only nine out of the twenty-four who had begun, but finally, the sun slipped beneath the horizon and those dancers were helped to their tents where they would be given water, only water at first, and in small amounts, so they didn't sick it back up until they were rehydrated. It is amazing to see how quickly people recover. First their eyes, dull, dry, and probably seeing everything as if through a haze, begin to regain a gloss and then a spark. Their backbones seem to stiffen and they sit upright, and then they are pouring down water and eating the food they are given like refugees from a winter famine.

Stella and I were invited to supper with the Lately family, and it was good and plentiful. Grandma Lately insisted that we take leftovers packed in recycled butter bowls. People were happy that the ceremony was over, that several people had completed their vow, but also because now the giveaways would begin. Most people who pledged to dance also pledged a giveaway for the last night. The goods that each dancer had collected throughout the entire previous year—blankets, small appliances, homemade quilts, nonperishable groceries, inexpensive jewelry and watches, hand-beaded belts and purses and earrings—all had been piled on folding tables or directly on the ground under the Sun Dance shelter. At a given moment, people were invited to line up and take something. It is a way of thanking people for supporting the dancer throughout the year as well as at the ceremony itself. As usual, the medicine people were given first place in the lines. Stella was beside herself to tell me something, and finally

I leaned over and she whispered in my ear, "Get that red Pendleton blanket, please!" I pushed her away with a smile, but I had it in mind to choose that blanket, except when I got to the table it was gone, and I noticed Ken Two Bears walking away with the Pendleton under one arm and a case of Coke balanced on his opposite shoulder. That's the way of it, to be expected. I chose instead a beautiful handmade star quilt in pastels rather than the usual primary colors. Stella would have to live with it.

Most people would spend the night at the campground, going home the next day, but I wanted to go home then. I trusted the neighbors to take care of the animals, but I was tired of the tension, the anxiety, the proximity of so many people in spite of the goodwill of most of them. It was over, and for it to be completely over until next year, I needed to leave the camp, to be home in my own bed.

Stella helped me pack up, take down the tent, and load everything in the pickup. She asked if Avril could come home and spend a few days with us, but she did not complain when I said no, so I wondered if she really wanted Avril there or had only asked because he wanted her to, and she didn't want to tell him no.

We drove the hour and a half home over back roads and then to the highway, where there was no traffic but a couple of cars probably coming back from the liquor store across the state line. As I turned off the highway, the moon disappeared behind clouds and the darkness enfolded us.

We passed the familiar line of trees at the north end of my property, almost invisible in the deep dark, like a line of giants saluting our homecoming. The cool evening breeze came damply though the open windows, bringing the promise of rain before morning, and I was doubly glad we had not stayed at the campgrounds. It would be a muddy mess there in the morning with everyone trying at once to get out of there.

The pickup came around the corner and the headlights swept

over the yard—a yard scattered with fluffy bumps, some dark, some white, some big as twenty-five-pound sacks of flour, some smaller with the edges waving in the breeze, and red—I noticed red. I stopped with the headlights shining on the porch where something big, white with red rivers run down it, was fastened to the door.

"Hazel," Stella said small. "What is it?"

"Someone," I started and choked on my words, had to begin again. "Someone has slaughtered our turkeys and our chickens."

5 Hazel

There are times when the mind must step outside the body, dis-associate itself, analyze as if it were another being altogether, mechanical, noncorporeal, and limbless, but beyond the body, beyond any humanity of emotions, only cold and logical. Of course, this is true, common knowledge, but I had to acknowl-edge that truth so that when mind and body reunited, I would not feel guilt for my lack of tears. *We had not been home.*

"STAY in the pickup," I said to Stella, and for once she did not seem inclined to disobey, but sat, eyes shocked wide.

I opened the pickup door. It gave that familiar complaining squeak as I pushed it past that little hesitation in the smooth arc of opening, a catch caused when the neighbor's bull rammed his head against it a year ago. That sound, so normal, should not ex-ist in this abnormal world, nor should those moths dance in the beams of the pickup headlights, nor the pickup motor purr as if there were no care in the world.

I have twenty-seven hens and two roosters—I used to have twenty-seven hens and two roosters, and while I did not count them, could not, since the pickup headlights picked out only a small area, I heard no nervous cackling off in the darkness, no sound at all except for the light wind fluttering and popping a dish towel I had forgotten on the clothesline just to the far side of the yard. Even the cats had gone into hiding; usually, they appeared the moment they heard the pickup motor, meow sharking around my feet, begging for me to milk the cow so they would have a lapping of that warm, sweet liquid.

No, I did not count the bodies, but most assuredly, all the chickens were dead. They lay in sad heaps of feathers, scribbles of blood defining where they had flung themselves in their death throes, some eviscerated, entrails shining in the headlight beam, trailing out from their slashed and smashed bodies. Something larger, white, decorated the front door. *We had not been at home.*

Not coyotes. I had lived here all my life, and never had coyotes attacked on this scale. They rarely hunted in packs, only the solitary animal taking an occasional foolish, independent spirited hen that had hidden out and not been shut into the coop at sundown. How had all these chickens managed to avoid being penned? I trusted my neighbors, knew they would have shut the chickens up in their coop, and clever as coyotes are, I never knew of one with opposable thumbs who could open a latched hen-house door.

It must be close to midnight. My neighbors would have done the chores close to sundown, which in these summer northern latitudes would not have set until close on nine o'clock. I bent and felt the body of a hen. Still slightly warm, I believed. Dead an hour, or maybe less. What instrument of death had been used? I thought, something like a sword, a machete, *mila haska*. Had they been shot first and then hacked up? Why the double murdering? Why mutilate the bodies? Why not take them to dress and eat? This was not the work of some hungry person, but some angry monster. *We had not been at home.*

What other acts of violence waited for me in the darkness, unseen and unexamined? I stared into the darkness, but the moon had not yet risen and I saw only vague outlines—the posts of the fence surrounding the garden were visible but not the wire; the broad, mottled outline of the rose bush but not the few roses in bloom; the loom of the low cow shed in the corral beyond but not the door; the square shape of the cow but not her eyes, not her accusing eyes. *We had not been home.*

Over the purr of the pickup motor I heard, as it was often possible to hear on clear nights, two miles away on the small feeder road to Highway 20 over into the edge of Nebraska, the motor of a truck laboring as it geared down for the climb up that long, long hill, just before the road crossed the state line. Out in the corral, the cow and her calf stamped their hoofs and switched their tails against the night-feeding flies and mosquitoes. Tomorrow I needed to spray them. She was a smart cow, but not too smart. She knew the hissing sound of the spray gun meant relief, and she would run toward anything that made that sound, even the cats hissing at each other in play. If she had been smarter, she would have known the advantage that humans have over animals, and not just advantage but responsibility as well. No sound at all came from inside the pickup. I looked down at Death lying at my feet, nudged Him with my toe, but He did not answer, not a sound.

I got back into the pickup, turned off the headlights, and switched off the motor. I reached over and pulled Stella close to me.

"Lie down and sleep," I said, and she did, her head sideways on the muscle of my thigh, her body curled onto the seat and her feet in worn, dirty white imitation Keds from a discount store in Rapid City hanging over the edge.

I tilted my head back and closed my eyes. Tulips, there must be tulips.

In an hour or less, the moon lifted over the horizon southeast, a small lantern of light in the night. I pulled Stella to a half-sitting position, half limp, got my right arm under hers, opened the pickup door and half pulled, half carried her, stumbling sleep-walking up onto the stone step, then the splintery rough wooden porch floor to the door, and there, there was that monstrous white thing fastened face-high on the outside screen. I opened the door, the weight of the object pressing down so the bottom of the screen door scraped against the wood floor of the porch, and Stella gave a little complaining moan. I shushed her, turned the key in the lock, and urged her into the kitchen.

In the bedroom, I pushed her over onto the bed, pulled off her shoes, and lifted her legs, covering her with the extra blanket from the foot of the bed.

The turkey had been crucified, wings stretched out to either side and nailed through. A wire encircled its neck, then went under the wings and up to a nail above its head, which hung down only a little, not limp and dangling like you might expect. The feet rested on the little wooden rail I had used to prop up notes for anybody who might show up when I had gone to town. The feet had been bent back a bit from the body, because, of course, a turkey is not flat like a photo, but long from front to back, even with the body turned a bit sideways like this one had been arranged. The feet had been crossed and a nail driven through, which could not have been easy to do with the turkey thrashing in its death throes and so little flesh and meat on the feet to drive the nail through.

The red-handled wire cutters were in the toolbox behind the pickup seat along with a dusty gunny sack, and I fetched those to the porch, held the screen door shut with my foot, and clipped the wire from around the turkey's neck. It was barbed wire. The turkey was heavy, so I had to take turns propping it up with alternate shoulders while I used the wire cutter to grasp and pull the nails that pinned its wings to the frame of the screen door. I had killed hundreds of chickens, wild ducks, pheasants, slit them open and pulled out their guts with my bare hands, dipped their bodies in hot water to make them easier to pluck, chopped off the heads and feet with a hatchet, washed them and cut them up and dipped them in flour and fried them up in a skillet. They were food. This turkey was innocent.

I placed it on the gunny sack shroud, wrapped it and took it to the pickup, placed it on the seat, rolled up the windows to keep the cats out, and replaced the wire cutters in the toolbox behind the seat.

I washed my hands in the cow's water tank and, leaning over, dabbed at my forehead first, then each of my cheeks. I took the suitcases from the back of the truck, carrying them inside, leaving the box of dishes, the ice chest, our small barbecue grill for later. The smell of cooked meat still lingered on the grill. It sickened me.

Big Ben ticked in my brown suitcase, the one I had found five years ago in the basement rummage store at Our Lady of Sorrows, only mildly scuffed; no one wanted it because it was locked shut and no key, but I picked the lock with a bobby pin. I had no need to lock it in the future that I needed it for anyway.

I opened it and put the clock on the table. Two-thirty in the morning.

I put fresh grinds in the coffee pot. Water still half filled the kitchen bucket, stale, but that would not matter, and I did not care anyway. I struck a match and lit the burner, and when the coffee had done, I sat at the table watching for the clock hands to move. I knew they would move, that they were moving, but for now, that was an act of faith without reason.

At five o'clock, as the sun warmed the horizon and lightened the kitchen, I heard Stella's tentative footsteps from the bedroom through the living room. Standing at the back of my chair, she put her hands on my shoulders.

I reached up and grasped her hands.

"Is it all right now?" she asked.

Is it right to lie to a child, even a not-quite child on the brink of adulthood? And how would I know whether I was telling a lie? Some things cannot be known, and we had not been at home.

"No," I said, but then, like a coward, I couldn't leave it at that. "But it will be," I added.

With the sky lightening in the east, we went to the shed for a spade to dig a grave, silence between us. The cats were at the bodies. One black cat, disembodied in the twilight of dawn, had a growling hold on the entrails of a speckled chicken, so that it appeared as if a pair of green eyes pulled the glistening gut.

Stella swiped at him with the spade on our way past, but he did not let go, took no notice, and we went on.

We first tried to dig beneath the box elder tree, but because of the hard, corky roots running just beneath the surface, we had to give that up, so we settled for a trench along the north fence inside the garden. I would plant flowers over all. Tilled over for many years, the spade slipped in easily. We took turns turning the soil, breaking up the big damp clods with our hands.

The sun sent searching rays over the carnage as we walked back to collect the carcasses, but there, by the passenger door on the pickup were the five turkey poults, very much alive and pecking at the door. They had grown to about the same size as the chickens, so I had assumed they were dead among the other bodies.

"Where did they come from?" Stella asked, a smile of delight on her face.

"That has always been the question," I responded.

She stooped, trying to catch them and hug them, but they hopped out of her reach, fanning their wings and uttering that croaking turkey talk as they returned to peck at the pickup door.

I was glad to see them, but not really surprised. Perhaps something of Stella's belief in the special nature of the mother turkey had been transferred to me and to her brood. I thought that four of the offspring were hens, one tom, so, incestuous as it might seem to someone not knowledgeable of animal breeding, there would be more chicks, another generation of this gift from who knew who or where. If the tom did not make it, I could always order a couple more from Norfolk hatchery.

"Stella, stop fooling around and help me," I snapped. I did not tell her that the white turkey's body was in the pickup. She had not looked for it among the chicken carcasses, probably assumed it was there somewhere. Once we got some of the chickens into the trench, I would set her to burying those while I brought the rest. No need for her to know about the turkey being in the pickup, or about the turkey being crucified on the screen door; those facts would only feed her fantasies.

The chickens had to be buried soon or the smell would become overpowering. We gathered them two at a time and carried them to the ditch grave in the garden while the turkey poults continued to peck and flutter around the pickup. I wondered if they knew their mother was inside or if they were only pecking at the door because of the sun glinting off the chrome door handle, an attraction to something shiny.

I thought I had twenty-seven chickens, hens, and roosters all counted, but there were twenty-eight bodies. The monster had killed what I had and even destroyed what I did not know I had. Except for the turkeys, but I did not feel they truly belonged to me or to Stella, but were their own owners, independent of us, hatched of the white turkey that had simply chosen to live with us for whatever reasons of her own. I did not think those reasons had anything at all to do with our worthiness as humans, but only that our place was the first the white turkey came across in her escape from whatever or her travel to wherever, and she had found a few kernels of grain on the ground that the chickens had missed, maybe something shiny on the screen door of the house that made her peck at it with no intention of knocking to call our attention to her presence.

The five poults had survived because they had inherited their mother's survival instinct, ran and hid themselves, and had not come out until hours after the noise of the guns and the squawking of the chickens had ended and whatever monster had done this had gone. For there had been shooting. I had seen shotgun pellets in the bodies, some spent pellets on the ground around some of the chickens. They were shot like wild birds, like fish in a barrel, if fish and fowl can be compared, and then they were slashed with a sharp knife as they flopped on the ground, or maybe, some of them did not move but only waited in death for the mutilation, the desecration.

I told Stella I was going to get the other spade. The young tom turkey had wandered off, but the four hen poults sat on the ground beside the pickup. I nudged them aside with a foot, opened the door. The gunny sack lay slack and empty on the seat. I stared at it, snatched it up and shook it as if a turkey could have miniaturized itself and hid in the folds. There it was, on the passenger side floor, and impossible to miss—a big white turkey with red blood on its feathers. I must have put it too close to the edge of the seat, and it rolled off onto the floor, but when I started to pick it up, it was warm, and I dropped it in shock. It let out a loud croaking sound, a distortion of a normal turkey cry, and the four hen chicks fluttered up into the pickup, perching on the seat, leaning over and calling. The white turkey stirred itself, but did not reply again.

I picked it up, pushed the poults aside, and perched myself on the edge of the door opening, pulling the white turkey onto my lap. It leaned against my chest, its sharp-clawed feet pressing into my leg. I could feel its heart beating, steady against my own side. I carefully probed its body with my hands. There seemed to be no broken bones, but there on the left side a wound, not deep, a shallow groove along its side that had bled considerably into its feathers and still oozed a little although it was mostly clotted and beginning to scab over. Around its neck, a cut where the wire had been, and other places beneath its wings where the wire had worn the feathers off showing pinky white raw marks.

Oh, gods. How would I explain this to Stella, what she would call another miracle of the sacred white turkey?

6 Hazel

The Kiefer brothers were good people; I told them that, and I told them that what happened earlier before Stella and I came back from the Sun Dance was not their fault, but even though our friendship and mutual neighborliness went back years to the previous generation of our parents, they could not overcome their guilt. They should have been aware that something was wrong, they said, when they brought us some young chickens as a gift, an apology. They heard the sound of distant gunfire, but they didn't think anything of it. Sounds carry, echo around these hills, so it could have been miles away. It could have been someone target practicing, popping cans with pistols or rifles or blasting who knows what for who knows why. This is a gun-ownership, gun-using community. People hunt year round, and many a kid had wild chicken in their lunch pails when it wasn't seasonal. Still, Albert and Ansel would not allow their guilt to be assuaged, and forever after, there would be a reserve beneath their friendliness, even years later when I would be asked to help serve dinner at the funeral of their nephew, killed when a tractor turned over on him and broke his neck.

And years later, people hearing the story for the first time are amazed that no one was caught and prosecuted. They have some notions that the sheriff should have found DNA or shell casings that should have been examined and pointed like arrows directly at the perpetrators. *Perpetrators.* Even that word was not used, unknown to us backcountry folk, Indian or white, in 1963. All that stuff comes from watching too much television, something I didn't have back then, and now that I do have, believe is best taken in moderation and with a dose of salt, sometimes with a pinch tossed over the shoulder to protect against evil, though I do it carefully when no one is looking.

Of course, I reported it to the county sheriff, and of course, he wrote it all down in that studious, careful way of his. He did not use a pencil that he licked before he wrote down the answer to each question, nothing so silly and hick as that, but in so many ways, Kenneth Wilkerson was the kind of small-town sheriff that you do see on television, a decent, honest man who tried his best to perform his duties, even if he was a little bit prejudiced against Indians, well, not so much prejudiced. I think, truth to tell, that he was a little afraid of us. He did come out to the house, looked around, examined the grave where I'd buried the chickens, took my word for how many there were, but there was nothing else to be done about it unless somebody walked into his office and told him flat out they had done it, and that was not about to happen.

He did ask me if I had pissed anybody off lately or even a long time ago, but I did not tell him about George. For what point would there have been? Nothing could be proved. George had been at the Sun Dance grounds when I left. I knew he was behind it, knew that he had sent Benny and probably somebody else that Benny knew to do it. I knew that's why Benny had faked his weakness and not completed his Sun Dance obligation. I knew at the moment Benny quit the Sun Dance that he was faking his faint. George wanted him out of the dance to go kill my animals before I got home. George could have used many methods of persuasion—maybe he knew something that Benny had done that could get him in trouble with the law or with his family, or maybe George had convinced Benny that he would put a spell on him if Benny did not do it. It does not matter, the result is the same—twenty-eight dead chickens and a crucified turkey, but one that some people would believe had risen from the dead, if I had been fool enough to let the story get around, which I was not.

I suppose George had not wanted it done earlier, the first night I was gone, the first night of the Sun Dance, because he wanted the kills to be fresh when I got home, although maybe not as fresh as they were. I think he did not think I would be leaving on the last night, did not expect me to get home until the next day. Benny and his helper, whoever that was, had probably only been gone an hour or maybe less before Stella and I pulled into the yard.

I knew that nothing would come of reporting it to the sheriff, but some things you just do as a matter of form, like setting the table with the fork on the left side of the plate. It does not matter, really; you can pick the fork up from a pile of cutlery in the middle of the table if you want to do it that way, but you do not. The fork goes on the left side of the plate. You report a crime to the sheriff. That is what you are expected to do, and if you do that, no one expects you to do anything else about it. So I made it look like I put the fork where it was supposed to go and left it at that. I had another matter to worry about, one that I might be able to do something about.

I still had title to the land my parents had gotten when the land had been divided up after the allotment act—well, actually, it was years after the act was passed because it took a very long time for the land to be surveyed, but people had known it was coming and most of them had picked the piece that they wanted and sat down on it with their family and relatives nearby. A good many people had been done out of their land in one way or the other over the years—that's how the Kiefer family got to be our neighbors and handed the land down to the two brothers, but my parents had not held it against them. They paid a fair price to the White Hawk family for it, and the White Hawks had in turn bought land over on Rosebud to be nearer kin they had there. My father had not been a drinker, so unlike many others, he had not been vulnerable to getting drunk and signing away his land for nothing. No, he was an early convert to Christianity, Catholicism to be exact, and much as I hold no interest in Christianity, I do acknowledge that my father's faith provided some protection against the vultures. He was taught to read and write by the missionaries who came here, became a valuable assistant for the Fathers, and learned a great deal of white man's ways, both good and evil, that made him wary of schemes, and although he lost his faith many years later, it did serve him for many years.

I love this land. I love the way the sun comes up over the low eastern ridge, a little north of that notch on top on the longest day of the year, and on the shortest day of the year, much farther south in the vee formed by another ridge a couple of miles to the east. In the winter, my ears hunger for the tune of the bees dancing over the milkweed flowers in the ditches, for the taste of rhubarb from my garden, baked up in pies with diamond shiny grains of sugar on top. The house is not much, three rooms in a row with the kitchen first and then the living room and then the bedroom. I am saving to put in a bathroom and a kitchen sink, but that cannot come for a few years, and except during the coldest winter days, I do not really mind the outhouse. People who have lived in the city all their lives cannot imagine the peacefulness of an outhouse or the satisfaction of watching a bucket fill with water as the windmill turns and pulls the water, cold and sweet, up a pipe from a hundred feet below. I suppose those people who enjoy going camping think they know what I am talking about, but there is a difference between playing at primitive living and living primitive. I do know this much: I have lived as if I was camping out most of my life, and when I have my bathroom and running water at a sink in the house, except for the Sun Dance, I will never camp out again.

Yes, I love this land, but I do not want to farm it, could not even if I wanted to. The tractors and the other equipment to farm it would cost so much for the little land that I have—and make no mistake, 160 acres of land is not much when the productivity is so low—that I would never make a living and always be in debt to the bank, paying off the interest every year at harvest and going deeper into debt to plant the next year's crop. No, I lease it out to Jack Olsen, a white man who leases several pieces of land, owns some other land that he bought from Indians over the years, and can afford to buy the equipment. I rarely have much to do with Jack, but we do pass the time of day in a friendly manner when we meet on the street. I suppose he is all right, never heard any awful stories about him, but we have nothing in common. Twice a year, he pays the standard lease fees to the tribal leasing office, and they pay it to me. That money, added to what I can earn from selling eggs and cream, and what I can grow in the garden and what people offer me for my services as a medicine woman and healer, that gives me a modest, a very modest, living, but I am bound to no one, punch no time clock, am glared at, not by un-reasonable supervisors at a job, but only by the cow when I am late to milk her. It is a good life. Or it was, until this massacre, this attack not only on me, but also on the animals that I have bound myself to care for.

It could be, I suppose, just George's jealousy that his reputa-tion as a medicine person is on the wane while mine is rising, but what Stella overheard at the Sun Dance campground made me believe there was more, and I could not contrive a plan to stop him until I knew what I needed to stop, but of course, as George was the head of the tribal leasing office, my lease to Jack Olsen passed through his office, and maybe that had something to do with it, although I could not imagine what.

Jack's lease payments—I knew he leased parcels of land from several other Indians not just me—came due on January 1 and July 1, and I knew that he paid them on time because I had always picked up my check around the fifteenth of January and the fifteenth of July, giving the tribal office time to process it, which I assumed meant that there was some page in an accounting book where they wrote down what was due to me from whom, when it was paid by that person, and then when the tribe passed the money on to me.

I always drove to the tribal offices and picked it up in person, but last December, I had gotten a letter from one of George's flunkies, Johnson Powers, who wrote to say that in future all lease payments would be mailed, citing the overcrowding and the inconvenience, the waiting, when so many of us showed up at the same time to get our payments. I did not like that idea. Too many things can happen between the intention and the fruition, so I had written back saying that I would still pick up my payment in person. It was not that bad to wait in line. I rather enjoyed it. You see the same people there every time, and you get to catch up on what is going on with their families, hear the latest gossip, you know. In a strange way, lease-payment days are a Lakota tradition. It reminds me of the old days that my parents told me about, the days when government food supplies that had been guaranteed to us by treaty were issued. They called them issue days, and part of the "issue" was beef, but not beef cut up and packaged, or even given out as whole sides, but issued as live animals, on the spot. It was a rare old good time, my father had said, smiling.

They drove the animals in from somewhere else, usually a few head here and a few head there from ranches over in Nebraska and then collected down at Merriman or Gordon and driven up to Pine Ridge in a long bawling line. It was dusty in the summer, trailing a fog of steam from the animals' warmth and breath in the winter. On issue day, the people would gather on the grounds surrounding the corrals; the agency clerks sat on the fence with their papers and lists in hand calling out the name of a Lakota family. The gate would be opened, the animal choused out with yelling and waving of hats, and the family who got the animal would run it down as if it were an old-time buffalo hunt. Once the animal was killed, other family members moved in to skin and gut the animal and cut it up. Of course, there was no refrigeration then, so in the summer the beef was cut into strips and hung on racks to dry for a few days in the sun, but some of the choicer cuts were cooked right then, and there was visiting and sharing with all the others getting their beef issue. The winter issue days were not as much fun because it was cold enough the meat would keep without drying, and the sun so weak that it would have taken weeks to dry anyway, so people went home as soon as the beef was processed. All of that stopped decades ago, but lease day is similar. There is no excitement of an animal run away through the crowd, kicking over drying racks and scaring children and old ladies, but lease payment day is its own kind of tradition. Sometimes exciting things happen, like the time at the January leasing payout two years ago when Rudolf Kills Crow got mad because he claimed other people were cutting ahead of him in line. He threw out an insult or two, and got an insult or two back, and before you know it, he and two or three other men were rolling around on the muddy tile floor, slugging each other in a half-effort way, hampered as they were by their heavy winter coats. It took a while to break it up because some people were encouraging the fight for entertainment and others were laughing too hard to break it up. Rudolf is a little, tiny, dried-up man about sixty years old, and the men he was fighting were not much better off, except for Tom Holder, who was big and pretty stout, but half blind and will not wear glasses, so he could not see three feet in front of him and kept slugging the door jamb next to Rudolf's head.

It is not just about the goofy stuff that happens though, or even the social value of seeing people you rarely see otherwise. I like to get my check put in the palm of my hand, not wait at home with a promise, a combination of those two old sayings: "The check is in the mail," and "I'm from the government, and I'm here to help you." I do not trust the mail, and I do not trust the government, federal, state, local, or tribal. Of course, I do not trust George, either, as the head and administrator of the lease program, but I was not really thinking about that because George does not really do any of the work anyway; his flunkies do. I wrote another letter telling the leasing office I would be in to pick up my check, and every month I got another letter saying my check would be in the mail, and I responded with another letter saying the same thing: I would pick up my check in person. Persistence usually works with any tribal official. I expected that when I went in to pick up my lease check on July 15, there would be almost as many people there as before the change in payment procedure, and the flunkies would cave in and give us our checks on the spot.

I was not even particularly upset about all this. Such things as this happen all the time when you are dealing with tribal officials or the Bureau of Indian Affairs, and nothing surprising about that when you think that most tribal government systems are modeled after the United States federal system and look at the breaking of the Christian's ten commandments that goes on up there, even though until recently, a lot of those offices had an oversized display of those ten commandments displayed in a prominent place. You can hear the sound of words and ethics being smashed all the way to the moon and back. Our tribe does the same thing; we just do it bilingual, throwing in a little breakage of traditional spiritual practice as well as Christian commandments, which makes iniquitous, illegal, immoral practices doubly double dealing.

Every person running for tribal council president campaigns on the idea that he—or she—is going to clean up the corruption, but of course it never happens, and no one believes it's going to, but that is the standard campaign promise the voter expects and always gets. Of course, the short—only two years—term of office for the TCP insures that no one can keep their promise to clean up the corruption. They spend the first year learning their job and the second year campaigning to keep it. The term should be four years.

Well, there I go, ennit? I implied that I did not mind the corruption, that it was expected and nothing to be done about it, and then I start thinking about how to fix it like you would think I was running for TCP myself. I suppose if you scratch beneath my surface, I am a bit of an idealist, but enough of a realist to know better. I believe in traditional spiritual practice, yes, mixed with a lot of practical practice like praying for a cure but taking your medicine, too, and sometimes that means herbal remedies and sometimes that means pharmaceuticals, much as I despise the prices and the lies those corporations put out. You have to be careful, but when all the fog is blown away, I believe in the One Commandment. That is not traditional, but as the Christians say, out of the mouths of babes.

Three years ago when Stella was only nine, she spent the night with the Lately family, and since they're Catholic, she went to mass with them the next day, and when she came home, she was asking me about the ten commandments. I tried to explain it to her as best I could, and when I had done, she looked at me and said, "That's just dumb. You only need one commandment: Don't be shitty."

I thought about that off and on for several days, trying to poke a hole in that logic, trying to think of reasons and situations where that one admonition would not suffice, and when I could not, I tried another approach. What if the person being shitty did not recognize that they were being shitty? I mulled that one over, steeped it in situations and situational ethics and decided that there are modern situations—rigging the stock market, for instance—where some people might not know that was shitty, like some isolated group living in the Amazon rain forest, but that speculation did not work because the rain forest people would never be in a situation to rig the stock market, only people who have access to the market through training for a job, and they would certainly know better. Rain forest people know about the ethics of their own community, and the same is true of every human group. So every human group knows, within their own ability to be shitty, what shitty is for them. Don't Be Shitty is a brilliant idea.

That winter, when we had a three-day blizzard and could barely make it through the snow in the yard to tend the animals and keep the fire going, let alone get through snow-drifted roads to town, I got down my box of fabric scraps, thread, and needles. Stella and I chose a pale pink print fabric, the remnants of an apron I had made. We cut a square piece and with bright purple embroidery thread we sewed on the words:

THE ONE COMMANDMENT
DON'T BE SHITTY

Stella had wanted to make the Don't Be Shitty part bigger and to use a different color of thread for the word "shitty," but I told her that would be unnecessarily emphasizing a vulgarity for the sake of humor, and I did not consider the statement a joke. She threw a little fuss but eventually let it go and, I think, is secretly proud when some person who pretends a sensibility they do not really own appears shocked to see that piece of work hanging on our living room wall above our battered old couch.

I would go to the leasing office on July 15 to collect my lease check, but I would not be shitty about it. In the months since the notices had come out that the checks would be mailed, I had been talking to other people about it, politicking them to follow my example and show up in person to get their checks. Some had asked, "What if we get the checks before the fifteenth, what then?" and my answer had been, "The letters said the checks would be mailed to us on the fifteenth. Have you ever known any tribal official to do anything on time, let alone early?"

There were two weeks to go, and the fourth of July was coming up with a community picnic at Jackson, a perfect opportunity to talk more people into going to the leasing office on the fifteenth.

On the weekend before, we were washing dishes when Stella asked if I was planning for us to be gone the whole day and to stay late for the fireworks show.

"Yes, I planned on it," I said. "You will not miss a bit of it, I promise."

But she stood there at some unease, holding the damp dish towel in her hand, a troubled look on her face, and I knew that was not the answer she wanted.

"Don't you worry about being gone so long?"

"You mean that someone might come and kill our animals while we are gone?" I handed her the cast iron skillet and she started to dry it.

"No, Stella, you know better than to dry the skillet. Put it on the stove and light the burner."

She nodded, and I knew she did not mean she understood that cast iron has to be heat dried to keep it from rusting.

I took her chin in my wet, soapy hand.

"Nobody is dumb enough to pull the same stunt twice," I said.

"They would be afraid of getting caught. They would be afraid that we might have someone stay here and watch the place while we are gone."

She pulled away, wiping her wet chin with the dish towel.

"Couldn't we do that? Get someone to stay here while we're gone?"

"Who would want to stay here and babysit turkeys on the fourth of July while everyone else is in town having a good time? Although you could stay home while I go to town," I said.

She might have done it, too, if I had allowed it, but small as the chance was of a repeat performance, I would not put my own grandchild in the potential path of danger. A surprised evildoer might do more evil than he originally intended.

"Couldn't we just tell people that someone is staying here to watch the place while we're gone?" she asked.

I waggled my left arm. Whenever I wash dishes, it seems like there is at least one fly who insists upon sitting on the point of my left elbow.

"And who would we say is doing this? And what would happen if the person we named then shows up at the picnic?"

She thought a moment, and a little smile came to her lips.

"Mr. Isenbert," she said.

"Mr. Isenbert? Your teacher? I thought he left last week to go visit his sister in Ohio."

"Yes," she said. "But not very many people know that."

I put the last plate in the second dishpan, went to the range for the teakettle.

"Step back," I said. "I do not want to splash you," and I poured boiling water over the dishes stacked in the pan. "Wait a minute to get the silverware out of the bottom, so you don't burn your fingers."

"I know," she said. "I've been doing this for years and years."

"So, are you saying we should tell a lie?"

"More like start a rumor," she said. She did not meet my eyes as she gingerly lifted a hot plate out and started to dry it.

I could not help it. I laughed.

So when we went to town for groceries, I made casual remarks to the three biggest gossips in town that Mr. Isenbert would be staying at our place on the fourth of July. It was believable. He was a shy man who never made close friends in the community. People said he had came out to this place so far from anywhere because his fiancée had left him at the altar. There was no more basis for that rumor than the one that we were starting, but small communities tell stories all the time, and rarely does a true one ever circulate. Sometimes it's necessary to be a very *creative* storyteller.

7 Hazel

Now that the Sun Dance was over, my medicine practice lightened up considerably, so I took over the chores that Stella had been forced to do before, and I knew she was grateful for the break although she had never complained about the workload. The night before the fourth of July, clouds built in from the west, filling the horizon with a slowly rising wall of black that climbed and climbed until it loomed overhead, threatening to collapse on everything below. Green lightning, at first intermittent, increased until the whole cloud bank seemed like some ancient smoke-blackened castle wall under siege of fire arrows, determined to topple. St. Elmo's fire danced on the guy wires of the windmill tower while wind increased and howled like a thousand demons throwing dust and pebbles through the air, scumming the surface of the milk in the pail as I hurried from the corral to the house, glad that I had done the milking and not Stella, whose skinny body would have been pushed here and there by the wind. The cow and her calf, due to be weaned soon, stood head down in the corner of the corral, sensibly staying outside the tin-roofed shed where they usually sheltered from ill weather.

As I turned the crank on the cream separator, the humming

of the machine could not be heard above the roar of the wind and the crash of the thunder, and just as I had finished, the rain came, at first in huge drops, each as much as a quarter ounce of water, I believed, flung down in the dust of the yard, and leaving a crater as they rebounded, shattered, and burst into dozens of smaller drops, and then, the deluge.

Stella, never one to be frightened of storms, stood at the screen door, feeling the water spray her face, sieved through the wire mesh, watching the lightning play through the downpour.

I got up, pulled her away, and shut the wooden front door.

"It is not safe," I said.

"I know," she said. "But it's so exciting!"

I left the pail of skim milk and the smaller can of thick yellow cream setting on the table then, and we stood, she in front and me behind, at the south-facing window over the wash stand and watched the huge old box elder, a trunk three feet across, swaying in the heavy wind from the west, bowing, as it seemed, away to the east, in subservience to a greater strength. Water poured in eddies and streams across the yard, pushing leaves, small twigs, and bits of debris ahead of it, flowing away to the lower places in the yard, eventually to sink into the water table and seep eastward to the Missouri and then down the Mississippi to the Gulf, and who knew from there? Maybe a drop of water that fell in my yard would join a thousand others and eventually wet the feathers of a penguin in Antarctica, be flung from that flightless bird's feathers into the air and evaporate to descend again as rain over China.

"Do you think the roads will be too muddy to go to town tomorrow?" Stella asked. "We might slide off in the ditch."

"If it looks like that, we can put some bales of hay in the back for weight to keep the rear wheels from slipping. We will go." I leaned forward a bit and kissed her clean, shampoo-smelling hair, damp from the wind-spun rain through the screen door, and I thought that I had to bend far less to kiss her every day, and soon, I might have to stand on a chair, and I thought, too, that size did not always mean a child needed less protection, only a different kind, a more difficult task than simply keeping them from falling down stairs.

We were up early the next morning, chores done, washed and dressed and out of the house and down the road in the pickup by eight in the morning, and need not have worried about muddy roads. The rain had run off through the sandy soil almost as fast as it came down, and only a few shallow puddles marred our road as we waved good-bye to the phantom Mr. Isenbert standing on our front porch with a shotgun.

Jackson is a border town; that is, it is a town right off the reservation. Most of the residents are white with a few Indians here and there living on the back streets and in the new housing addition south of the main town, but day visitors are both Indian and white, both coming to town to do their shopping, to sit on the bleachers at the livestock auction and gossip, and sometimes, on holidays, both participate in an uneasy mix, like oil floating on water, both present and together, but only proximate. The town bustled with people who had gotten up earlier than we did. Main Street had been repaved two weeks ago, and for the first week, cars were made to park at the curb to help smash down the asphalt, and this week they were made to park in the middle to make sure it got smashed down equally from curb to curb, but since people were not used to parking in the middle and there was no striping to mark out spaces, cars were parked higgledy-piggledy, some taking up more space than they deserved and everybody grumbling about it to each other as part of their first greeting.

"Good day to you, Mrs. Phelps. Ain't it a shame the way they make us park our cars? Always some folks that can't figure out the angle to pull in and take their share of the parking spot out of the middle of two. I don't know why they decided to do this right now. Why couldn't they of waited until the fourth was over? How you doing, by the way?"

Already the temperature had reached ninety degrees and climbing, and heat waves had begun to shimmer over the streets, reviving the acrid smell of the newly laid asphalt, which the rain had dampened the night before, and after the parking problems, the rain was the next topic of conversation.

"Got forty-five hundredths at my place. 'Course, that's with the new free rain gauge the co-op sent me last year along with the calendar. It ain't near as accurate as my old one, but the kids got to playing with it last fall and busted it. I swear, we got at least another hundredth that the gauge didn't show. My neighbor says . . ."

The older women wore pastel print dresses and looked askance at the younger women and teenagers in jeans and shorts, and the men who thought of themselves as ranchers wore jeans and boots and snap-front western shirts and wide-brimmed cowboy hats, while the farmers wore bib overalls in the Sunday-best striped color rather than the solid indigo ones, with new blue chambray shirts underneath and clean but worn lace-up boots and droopy brimmed straw hats. Some of both wore gimme caps from the Farmer's Co-op or the local feed mill. Some of the more modern men wore no hats at all. The Indians wore whatever they had with no regard to what they considered their primary occupation. Whatever the clothes, everyone sweated in the humid heat, and old ladies wiped their faces and their grandchildren's faces with clean, white pressed hankies.

The Club Café was open and full of people but no one was eating, only drinking iced tea, because the picnic was in the dusty city park at noon and everyone was saving their appetite for the barbecue the town provided and the side dishes that everyone had brought from home, and no one worried a moment about getting botulism from potato salad with mayonnaise left too long without refrigeration, and no one did get sick except those little kids who ate too much of the ice cream that came after the main meal.

I met Sally Tunstall and Joann Reece, two women I had known years on end, fellow boarding school students, and now adult women with grandchildren, and the three of us sat in the café and through the big plate glass window, we watched people walking by and clotting in clumps on the corner to talk while other annoyed people had to walk around them to cross the street. Stella had run off with the Lately children and a group of others from her school with the promise that she would "check in" with me from time to time and show up at the park to eat, and not get into cars with older kids and go driving around.

The stores were open, the hardware, the grocery, Jackson's Five and Dime, and people wandered in and out, looking but not buying anything. They would close at noon, and open later on when some folks who did not care to stay and watch the fireworks might want to buy their groceries or some other odds and ends before they went home.

At eleven-thirty, we gave up our booth in the café and started toward the park, in a general exodus from the three blocks of Main Street. Even without a watch, anyone could tell it was about time to eat because the deep pits where the two steers had been cooking for twenty-four hours had now been opened and the air was filled with the smell of cooked meat, and according to custom, members of the volunteer fire department would be cutting up the meat, or, rather, gathering it as it fell off the bones, putting it on huge serving platters.

Joann and Sally went off to round up their husbands and children and grandchildren, and I walked on until Stella joined me, breathless and sweaty and swinging on my arm and begging to go sit with the Lately family to eat. I insisted that she get in line with me first so I could make her put some vegetables on her plate and not just sweet Jell-o fruit salad and cake and a few bites of shredded beef.

Too late to hold back without being obvious, I saw that Ruby Denison and her sister, Pearl, would be in line right ahead of me. They were not bad women, but if they could help it, they never, never let themselves stand out of the way of anything free, and their tendency to the lowest sort of gossip was even more odious.

Everyone in small communities gossips; it is a form of entertainment where higher forms may be absent, and I like to hear it and tell it myself, but I believe that passing on of information heard, with the preface "so and so told me" or "I heard," was the deepest a person should go. Ruby and Pearl dredged even deeper into speculation about the subjects of such gossip, enlarging upon the situations and those persons' characters, and they did it with such a show of innocent knowledge, nodding of heads, whispering breaths of conversations, alternating with louder words spoken in disapproval, which the listeners inevitably passed on as truth.

It was not the passing on of information of a dubious nature that bothered me, no, it was the embroidering of the stories that turned the ordinary mistakes of ordinary people, mildly interesting, into dramas performed by people who were Jezebels, Don Juans, or worse, for it was gossip of a prurient nature that delighted them the most. But the ladies had seen me; I could not well turn away without making an obvious snub that would be enlarged upon and told to everyone in the county before midnight.

"Oh, no, Hazel, there's—" Stella said, but I interrupted her with a shush and an elbow nudge and never faltered in my progress toward the food line with Ruby and Pearl at the end.

"Hello, ladies," I said, smiling as if they were just the company I desired most. "That barbecue beef sure smells wonderful."

I tried to keep the conversation light, and it did run on in that vein for some time, with interruptions to shout hellos to other friends and acquaintances, but the line snaking up to the serving tables was long and full of people who were worthy of a story, and eventually, I had to take notice of Ruby's—or Pearl's—lifted eyebrow and glance or knowing nod. I saw the Latelys in line behind us and sent Stella to join them, knowing that nudges and nods would develop into the full-blown stories as soon as the line had passed the presumed offender. No sense in Stella and me both suffering.

And, of course, I knew that eventually the sisters would work their conversation around to an inquisition about the bloody destruction of my animals. I knew they were only waiting until we sat down over our plates to begin the inquiry, when they could be reasonably sure that I would not get up and walk away from them.

The Jackson Volunteer Fire Fighters dished out the barbecue, generous portions of rich, smoked meat with buckets of barbecue sauces marked MILD, MEDIUM, and HOT!!! I heard someone ahead of me in line joke about needing the fire department there to douse anyone that that the sauce set on fire, and saw Joe Sanders's grim little smile in response, sure that he had already heard the joke several times and would hear it several more before the line ended.

I took a generous serving of barbecue, potato salad, baked beans, green salad, a slice of crusty bread, a piece of chocolate cake, and a large paper cup of iced tea, and watched as Ruby and Pearl took several slices of bread and arranged them on the edges of their plates like sideboards so the plates could hold more food.

We were lucky to find a picnic table unoccupied on the far side of the park beneath one of the trees still struggling to grow up. The park was only five years old, and so were the trees, of course, and the city had planted Chinese elms, a very hardy tree and fast-growing for northern climes, but even a Chinese elm tree took time. Therefore, the park had an adolescent look, spindly trees with limbs about to shoot out of their shirt sleeves and pants legs, but spotty. Most families had ignored the trees and brought big umbrellas for shade and blankets to sit on the ground. The park slanted a bit from west to east, and the trees on the east side had been winter killed, leaving an opening to a field where the fireworks show would be held later. A small stage sat on the northeast end, just before the food tables and angled slightly to face the main area of the park, with a microphone and speakers set up.

The mayor, a short, fat man with a sweating face that he kept mopping with a handkerchief, stepped up to the mike, which squealed in protest, and the crowd laughed a little. He mopped his face and grinned nervously, began again.

"Welcome, everyone, to the tenth annual Jackson Fourth of July Picnic."

Everyone cheered as best people can when their mouths are full of food.

"You know," Ruby started to speak in a low voice, leaning toward me, but got interrupted.

"Thanks to the Jackson Commercial Club for sponsoring this event and to the Jackson Volunteer Fire Fighters for barbecuing the beef, and to all of you good folks who brought food for the potluck."

More cheering, still half volume.

Again, Ruby leaned toward me, but before she could say anything, the mike squealed again, and people groaned and held their ears.

"Sorry, folks," the mayor said. "It hurts me as much as it hurts you. I'll turn off this noisy thing in a minute. I just wanted to say that there will be our usual games after dinner, so don't eat too much if you want to win the sack race or the foot race or take part in one of the softball games. We still have room, so if you want to sign up, come up here and Miss Reynolds will take your names down." He nodded at a cute little blonde high school girl sitting at a card table at the end of the stage. "The games will end around five o'clock; then, if anyone wants to, the food will be left out for a pick-up supper, and the fireworks show will start as soon as it's dark, which, I'm told will be around 8:45, so stick around for that. In the meantime, enjoy your food, and don't forget to sign up for the games. We've got some pretty good prizes donated. You might want to think about that." He hooked the mike back on the stand, where it gave a good-bye squeal, and he stepped away.

"You know," Ruby said, "he talks about cleaning up this town."

"Really?" I said. "I didn't hear him say anything except to sign up for the games and enjoy our food."

She slapped me on the arm. "Not now! I mean in the city council meetings. And it's been in the newspaper."

Pearl nodded vigorously. "That's right."

They were looking at me expectantly, so I obliged them.

"Clean up the town how?"

"Well," said Ruby, "he said there's too many drunks on the streets on Friday and Saturday nights. You know, annoying for people to see, and some of them accost the ladies and children."

"I never saw much of that," I said. "Of course, I come do my grocery shopping during the day and go home at night."

"Speaking of that," Pearl started, and I knew that I had left them the opening to quiz me about the chicken massacre at my place, and I wished I had just nodded and looked interested.

Ruby nudged Pearl. "Not now! We'll talk about *that* later. I'm telling her this other thing." She looked at me as if I was supposed to make further inquiries. I took another bite of baked beans.

"These could do with a bit more molasses," I said.

Ruby pressed her lips together and stared at me, but only for a minute, and then she went on.

"Well, he talks about cleaning up the town, so he got the city to put a midnight closing on the all the bars in town, and the cops are supposed to arrest anyone who even looks like they might be tipsy."

"So, how do they get all the Indians packed into the city's one little tiny jail cell?" I asked.

"What?" she said, and then she got it.

"Well, that's what I'm talking about!" she said. "They've been arresting Indians just for being in town, just for walking down the street."

This was old news to me. The city could not afford to hire people to help work on city garbage collection, so they arrested Indians on the pretense that they were drunk, and when the Indians could not pay their fines, they were sentenced to thirty days in jail and forced to work as city garbage collectors—and gardeners for this very city park and whatever else the city needed. The tribe complained, threatened to tell people to boycott Jackson businesses, but the truth was that Jackson was the only place to buy groceries and whatever else was needed for fifty miles around. Many Indian people didn't have dependable vehicles to drive a long distance to buy what they needed. Jackson city officials knew the tribe's boycott threat was empty, so Indians were still arrested by the city to provide free labor.

"HE didn't get arrested," she said.

"Who?" I asked.

"HIM! HIM! The mayor!"

"Why would he be arrested?" I asked.

"Well, a week ago on Saturday night he got drunk in the VFW Club. It's in the basement, you know, underneath the regular VFW meeting hall. And then he was too drunk to walk, so he was crawling up the steps and trying to look under the skirts of women, going up and down and grabbing at their ankles."

I could not help but laugh. The image of the round mayor playing grabby with the legs of some of the ladies in town was funny.

"You laugh," Pearl said accusingly.

I restrained myself with difficulty.

"So the cops came, but they didn't put him in jail. They picked him up and put him in the cop car and took him home. No garbage truck detail for him!"

"That is not really fair," I said mildly, but I was angry. Until I thought about it a moment longer. The story might be true, or it might be something the sisters had made up, but it had distracted them from asking me about the other thing, but no, it had not.

"Speaking of going home," Pearl started again. "I heard about that chicken crucifixion at your place." Ruby didn't stop her this time.

I almost choked on my chocolate cake.

"What?"

"The crucifixion! You know. Where somebody came and killed your chickens and nailed that one up on your door!"

That she said "chicken" and not "turkey" did not surprise me. These two often got their facts wrong, sometimes I thought on purpose to make a better story, but this time I thought it was a genuine mistake because crucifying the white turkey was far more interesting and ominous. But Pearl had said *crucifixion*! Nobody knew that part, not even Stella, only me and whoever had done it.

"Who told you that?" I demanded.

Pearl blinked. "Why, everyone was talking about it," she said.

For the first week after it happened, everyone was talking about it, and when I went to town I was stopped every few steps by someone wanting to comment to me about it, to get the exact details, to make ain't-it-awful statements, but that was almost three weeks ago now. True, this was the first time I had seen Ruby and

Pearl since the incident, but that was not the point. No one else had mentioned crucifixion.

"*Who* told you that?" I said again.

"Well, I don't know," Pearl looked sideways at Ruby, who was mopping up beans on her plate with a piece of bread. "Sister, do you remember?"

"No," Ruby said without looking up. "Just someone said."

I grabbed Ruby's wrist and held it. She looked up with a jerk, eyes wide, tried to pull her hand free and gave up, the piece of bread dropping onto the table. While Ruby and Pearl were gossips of the worst kind, adding details that did not exist to make a story juicier, neither of them was likely to come up with the crucifixion angle, not on their own, not in a million years. Whoever told them the story knew who did it, had heard the story from that person, or was one of the people who did it.

"*Who* told you?" I repeated.

"Hazel, you're hurting me," Ruby said. And when I did not let go, she said, "I guess someone at the grocery store, maybe a week or so ago. Do you remember that, Pearl?"

"Nooo. People tell us things all the time. It's hard to remember who said what."

I dropped Ruby's hand. Stupid to push them. They would not remember; I believed them, and whoever told them knew that as well as I did. Telling them the true story of it so it would get back to me was another attempt to scare me, to keep alive that feeling of violation and violence and the potential for more. I had no need to scare old ladies, even silly ones like Ruby and Pearl. It is like arguing with a fool. My father said never do it. He said people walking by will wonder which one is the fool. Better to ignore them and avoid them.

I got up and picked up my plate.

"I have to find Stella," I said. "I will see you later."

Ruby picked up the fallen piece of bread from the table and

took a bite. A cruising fly lit on the baked bean sauce that had gotten on the table top.

Why did I care who told them what? I knew it came from George Wanbli and his people; I did not need confirmation.

I walked over and put my empty plate, napkin, and plastic fork in the trash can, looking around for the Lately family and Stella.

Behind me I heard Ruby holler at Ellie Anderson walking by.

"Ellie, when is your baby due?"

Ellie was a big woman with a voice to match.

"I'm not pregnant," she said, quietly for her.

I looked at Ruby and Pearl exchanging knowing little smiles.

"Haven't told Walter, yet, huh?" Ruby said.

Ellie took a couple of steps toward them. "I said I'm not pregnant!" Now people were turning to look. Ruby and Pearl didn't say anything, but Ruby's smile got bigger.

"Here," Ellie said. "See the public restroom over there?" She pointed to the cement block toilets on the far side of the park, and her voice climbed louder yet. "Why don't you and I just step into the bathroom and I'll *prove* to you I'm not pregnant!"

Ruby's smile faded. Both she and Pearl seemed to shrink a bit. People around them were murmuring now.

"Are you coming with me? I can prove I'm not pregnant!" Pearl leaned her big hands on the table in front of the two women; they leaned away from her. Ellie stood up, hands on her hips. "I didn't think so," she said, and walked away, taking long steps. "Goddamned busy bodies," she said to herself.

Yes, I thought, they were, but useful for some people's purposes.

8 Hazel

After the fourth of July, I had little time to ruminate over who told the crucified turkey story to Ruby and Pearl and what that telling could mean, and what might be lying in wait around some future corner. The Sun Dance in late June may be the high point of the year for most Lakotas, the culmination of a year's preparation for the ceremony, and the timing of it—traditionally at the summer solstice—does chronologically mark the middle of the year, but for me, the high point comes later on, in the summer in July and August, when every plant rushes to bloom and fruit; even the air reaches a full, thick ripeness, sounds seem deeper and rounder; and tomatoes dusted off, sprinkled with salt, and eaten directly from the plant leave a tang on the tongue that is never attainable from winter tomatoes preserved in a jar. And preserving was what I did in the high summer.

Although the tomatoes would not be ripe until later in the month, there were herbs to be picked and dried, both medicinal and culinary, the wild ones from the ditches and fields and the domestic ones grown a purpose in my garden. The cucumbers were coming on ready to be picked and put down in pickling crocks, carrots and early root crops ready to be pulled and stored in the coolness of the cellar for winter. Jars had to be retrieved from the shed, the spider webs brushed off, the jars washed and sterilized in boiling water, ready to put up green beans, tomatoes, and pickle relish. In August, the wild plums and chokecherries would ripen, and there would be days of standing over a hot stove stirring pots of bubbling fruit and hoping it would jell without adding another package of pectin. That would come later, but there was plenty enough and more to do now in the ten days before I would go to the tribal leasing office.

Stella and I were up early every day, and as soon as the cow was milked, the cream separated, the turkeys and what I referred to as my new chickens fed, we set to washing vegetables picked late the night before or early in the morning and packing the whole or chopped vegetables in jars for the canner, timing it and lifting the hot jars out onto tea towels spread on the table, listening for the satisfying POP as the jar lids sealed one by one, counting the pops to make sure they all sealed. I wiped the sweat from my forehead with the tail of my apron and thought about the winter, when we would eat this food and rest from putting it up. Stella helped, of course, as I had helped my mother and as her friends were obligated to help their mothers. In another month, toward the middle of August, the fruit trucks would start arriving at the cattle auction barn on Wednesdays, bringing peaches, apricots, and plums grown farther south in Nebraska and brought up here, where most of us could not get a domestic fruit tree to survive through the winter. I always bought a bushel of peaches to can, or apricots, or, in years when I had less money, half a bushel or a flat to make jelly and jam supplementary to that made from chokecherries and wild plums picked for free.

The turkey poults had grown, the four hens bullying the one tom and all of them competing with the chickens for feed and chasing the kittens that tumbled and played in the early morning and lay panting in the shade during the hot afternoons. The white turkey had recovered completely as far as I could tell, and now all of them looked like the ordinary turkeys that I knew they were, and Stella could never be induced to believe.

The stream of other people who believed the white turkey was holy had dropped off before the Sun Dance, but now the parade resumed with the story of the crucified and resurrected turkey being spread by Ruby and Pearl and everyone else with a loose tongue and a desire for something awe inspiring and horrific. Usually visitors arrived in the late afternoon, not during the day because, they, too, were busy canning and preserving whatever came in from their gardens, but almost every evening right after supper, a car or two would come down the driveway through the gathering twilight, doors open and people get out, stretching and saying their hellos. Everyone knew by now that I disapproved of turkey worship, so they did not ask to see the turkey, but I knew the reason that most people visited. Since they arrived about time to shut the chickens and turkeys up for the night, I accommodated their desire to see the white turkey by asking them to walk around with me while I shooed the straggler hens and turkeys into the coop and shut the door. They expected something more than ordinary poultry, and some of them would probably have been happy to pick up the turkey and feel for her stigmata, but I did not mention the extraordinary nature of the white turkey's survival, and they knew better than to make extraordinary comments. I thought I went far enough for them. There was never any repeat of the Latelys' experience of seeing the white turkey silhouetted against the fence with the crown of barbed wire.

Sometimes the visitors brought cold soda pop to share, and sometimes I served iced tea, and we would all sit under the box elder tree, slapping at the occasional mosquito and watching the fireflies dance over the alfalfa that Jack Olsen had planted on the fields I leased to him. I enjoyed company, enjoyed hearing the homely stories of their lives as much like mine. Sometimes a visitor would bring a gift and ask for a meeting on another day about a problem they had, a health problem usually, but sometimes about an anxiety or a personal conflict with another person that they needed advice to resolve. Sometimes I accepted their gift, and if we were alone with no other visitors, I brought out my pipe and conducted a ceremony. Sometimes I felt that their problems were something that they should work out themselves without asking for spiritual intervention, and then I refused their gift as gently as I could with advice that came from my purely human perspective. Sometimes the latter strategy worked as well or better than a ceremony. I often think that if I was a spirit, I would appreciate being consulted from time to time, but I would get rather annoyed with those people who cannot seem to wipe their noses without advice.

The days passed quickly, a happy routine that I sometimes hoped would continue in this way always, hard work but rewarding, the warmth of the sun, the smell of good earth beneath my hands, the occasional rain, the company of friends in the evenings. It was, I knew, a sort of limbo that gives peace and stability, but one that is not healthy to wish would last forever.

I promised Clara Lately that she could have whatever she wanted to harvest out of my garden if she would come stay with Stella for the day while I went to the tribal leasing office. The Latelys owned land too, but it was not rich enough for wheat farming, only for grazing, and that did not bring in as much lease money, so they ran a few head of cows on it themselves. Clara brought the kids, except for her older daughter, Nancy, who did not want to hang around with the younger kids anymore and had never been much help with the summer work anyway. I had no idea what might happen at the leasing office, so I did not want Stella along, but I did not want to leave her home alone, either. I knew that with the stink I had been making about picking up my lease money in person, several people would know I would not be home on the fifteenth of July, and one of them for sure, as the head of the leasing department for the tribe, would be George Wanbli. No sense in taking chances.

The drive to the tribal leasing offices would have been pleasant if I had not been thinking ahead about what might happen, and if a big bumble bee had not flown in the window and stung me on the cheek before I could even think about it. It was not his fault, but I was angry at him just the same, and it hurt; it really hurt, and I killed the bee when I reacted by slapping it away. I had no herbs with me, which I use along with a paste of soda and water to take out the sting, so I just drove on, feeling my cheek swelling up into my eye.

The parking lot at the tribal office building was full, but usually on lease payment days the lot would be full and cars would be parked for a block up and down the street. Some people must have decided to accept the mailed payment, but there was still a line inside, fifteen or so people ahead of me, mostly older folks who did not like change. I tried to talk to Lily Rousseau ahead of me in line, but she was very old and mostly deaf, so it was slow going even with the help of her daughter-in-law, Loretta, who had brought her and who clearly was not very happy about having to do it.

The old lady motioned at my face.

"What happened?" she asked, very loud. I suppose if you cannot hear yourself speak, you do not know how loud you are talking.

"Bee sting," I said.

"Beastie?" she asked, her rheumy eyes fixed on my cheek. She had to look up a long ways. She was less than five feet tall.

"BEE STING," I repeated.

"Well, I wouldn't put up with that," she said indignantly. "I'd hit him right back."

I exchanged a puzzled look with Loretta, who had an exasperated little smile.

"She can't see very well, either," she said. "She thinks you have a black eye."

Lily pulled on the sleeve of Loretta's blue-checked cowboy shirt.

"I want a purple pop," she declared.

Loretta said, "She means a grape pop."

"Go ahead," I said. "There's a pop machine around the corner in the employees' lunchroom. I will stand in line with her."

Loretta did not want to run any new errands, I could tell, but she went down the hall, fumbling in her black handbag for change.

The tribal secretaries in high heels walked past, chewing gum and staring at us like they usually do. Some of them were honest, hard-working women, but the newest hires had gotten their jobs in the usual way, nepotism, and did not expect that they would have to do any real work so they did none, and since it was the usual practice, nobody paid them much attention.

The door to the leasing office some twenty feet up the hall was open, of course, but it seemed to take a long time for each person to get through the door and get to talk to anyone. I suspected that people were being told to sit down in the two or three chairs inside and wait, and that was it, a pretty common tactic. If you make people wait long enough, pretty soon most of them get tired and go away and then the bureaucrats only have to deal with the two or three really persistent ones, who are treated first to a long conciliatory conversation that begins with the history of the office, proceeds to the past policies, moves on to the necessity for changes in policy and the value of these new policies for making things run more efficiently. If the listener has not been lulled into a soporific coma by that time, the official gets up, opens the door, thanks the complainer for his/her concern, leads them out, and shuts the door behind them. If the listener is still awake and refusing to move, then the official's speech turns to lecturing like a priest in confession who had just heard the same parishioner admit to their twenty-fifth incident of adultery. If that lecture does not shame the complainer into leaving, then the official resorts to the angry speech threatening to call the police, which usually gets the complainer out of the office—unless the complainer's cousin happens to be a tribal policeman. In that case, the official simply disappears into the back of the office, leaving the complainer sitting until the complainer leaves and the janitors come in to sweep up.

I think that the leasing official was still at stage one: make everyone wait.

The clock at the end of the hall registered eleven o'clock. I had been in line for an hour and a half and would have to leave for the bathroom in a few minutes. Only five more people had joined the line behind me. I knew that the official would leave for lunch early, probably in another half hour, not to return for at least an hour and a half, partly because that is the usual practice of any tribal employee above janitor rank, and partly because he would hope that the waiting line of people would get hungry, leave, and not come back. It was a strategy that usually thinned out the number of people waiting to complain by at least half.

Fifteen minutes later I went to the bathroom, and as I was washing my hands, I saw myself in the mirror. The left side of my face was very swollen although it no longer hurt, and my hair, which I had pinned up so carefully this morning, had been stirred by the breeze through the open pickup window, and now straggling wisps fell about my face. My white blouse sported a dark brown wet stain, too. The soda machine had been out of the purple stuff; Loretta had brought a cola, which had exploded upon opening and shot a volcanic spume down the front of me. I looked squalid.

At 11:25 I walked past the people in line ahead of me and through the door of the leasing office. A small windowless office, it had a chest-high counter dividing it down the middle with a half door at one end leading into the small area where an older woman—one of the real working women, Mary Denison, niece of Ruby and Pearl—sat at a desk and behind her, another door with a translucent glass window and letters painted on it in a curve: Johnson Powers, Tribal Leasing Chairman. Oh, yes, I knew him, cousin to Benny Dismounts, one of George Wanbli's acolytes from the Sun Dance, and was not that a connection to think about?

In front of the counter, four chairs with seats and backs upholstered in orange plastic ranged against the wall, all filled with weary-looking people, three men and one woman, people I knew remotely, but not well, and above them the usual posters on the wall. One of them announced opportunities to apply for small business grants, but the deadline for submission had passed six months earlier. The front of the counter was dirty knee-high from people who had propped muddy boots against it while waiting, and on top, a pen with a chain in the end fastening it down. It was probably out of ink.

"I need to speak with Mr. Powers," I said to the secretary, who sat with her back half turned toward the counter, I knew, because she wanted to look too busy to be bothered.

She turned reluctantly toward me. I felt sorry for her, knowing that she had to perform this charade several times a week and sometimes several times a day, but she managed it as well as she could.

"Mr. Powers is busy at the moment," she said. "Could I help you?"

"I am Hazel Latour. Here to pick up my lease payment."

"I'm sorry," she said, "but the new policy is to mail those checks."

"Have they been mailed yet?" I asked.

Her eyes darted sideways; she pursed her lips, released them, and swallowed. I knew she was not expecting that question.

She stood up and said, "I'll just check on that for you."

"Oh, no. I'll just ask Mr. Powers myself," I said and pushed open the half door into her little domain and stood in front of the door to Powers's office, my hand on the knob.

She took a half a step backward, her foot in its sensible shoe catching on the leg of her chair, which rolled slightly away from her.

"You can't go in there!" I saw her eyes take in my swollen face, the general squalor of my hair and clothes.

"I will only be a minute," I said. "I can save you the trouble of mailing my check."

She hesitated, and in that moment I turned the doorknob and walked into Johnson Powers's big office with a window in the opposite wall and light from it falling on his oiled black hair. He had his back turned as he wrote on something on a table off to one side of his desk.

"I'm about done with this, Mary," he said without turning.

Mary had recovered herself and stood immediately behind me in the open door.

"Oh, Mr. Powers, I'm so sorry!"

Powers turned around swiftly, took in my less than neat appearance, and stood up.

"Mary, I've told you to call the tribal cops when drunks show up."

"I'm sorry, sir," she started, but I interrupted her.

"I have not been drunk in more than twenty years," I said to Powers. I knew him vaguely, had seen him at meetings and just around, but I was sure he would never remember ever seeing me, and might not have recognized me in my present condition even if he had seen me before.

"Well, well," he said, raised his hands a little and lowered them again against his sides.

I said nothing. I know a little psychology myself, know that if you want to make someone uncomfortable, do not respond when they expect you to, or the way they expect you to. So I just stood there. And so did Mary. And so did Johnson Powers.

I turned around and gently pushed her out of the office.

"It's fine, Mary," I said, and shut the door behind her.

Powers, recovering himself somewhat, said, "See here, you can't just barge in here. I'm about to go to lunch."

"I doubt if you will starve in the next few minutes," I said as I seated myself in the leather chair in front of his desk. He turned a little and stared at me, unsure of what to do next. I noticed that his shirt had two buttons undone right over his belly.

"Please," I said with an expansive gesture, "Have a seat. What I have to discuss will only take a few minutes and then you can get to your lunch or whatever." I glanced at the table. "Whatever you were doing when I came in."

A look of wariness, caution, crossed his face. He glanced at the table where he had been working, took a step toward it, looked at the other door that led directly into the outside hall without going through the secretary's anteroom, then checked himself, walked behind his desk, and sat down, but only on the edge of his chair.

"What do you want?"

"What do people usually come to your office twice a year on the fifteenth of the month to do?"

His eyes got big, eyebrows raised. "How do you know—" He started to say, and then he tumbled to what I meant and his eyes narrowed again.

"You know very well that our policies have changed, that all lease payments to tribal members are going to be mailed from now on. You've been told repeatedly in letter after letter."

"Yes," I said, "and I have told you repeatedly in letter after letter that I would be here on the fifteenth of the month to pick up my lease payment in person. And from the looks of that line outside, I am not the only one."

"The checks have already been mailed," he said, but his eyes would not meet mine, glanced to the side, and I did not believe him.

"No. They have not, and I want mine now." I said it quietly, matter of factly, a simple statement.

He pressed his hands down on his desktop.

"They have already been mailed," he repeated.

"No, they have not. Are they out there in file cabinet?" I nodded my head toward the outer office.

He did not answer my question.

"What's your name?"

"Hazel Latour," I said, settling myself more firmly in the chair.

He pushed himself back deeper into his chair, tilted back a little, hands on the deeply padded arms.

"Well, Hazel," he said. "This office is part of the Oglala Lakota Nation under the auspices of the Bureau of Indian Affairs, who have final say in all such matters, as has been the case since the tribal government was instituted in its present form after the Indian Reorganization Act. Since then, the tribe has elected a series of tribal council chiefs and members to represent the people, in accordance with the original regulations and by laws set out and approved by the Bureau under its representative here. In the years since, we have continued to serve the people . . ." He went on. I let him go on for a while.

"You're going to be late for lunch," I said.

"What?"

I thought he might be like some people who cannot continue their train of thought if they are interrupted in the middle. For some people, if you ask them to continue the alphabet beginning with M, they cannot do it. They may pretend they can, but you can see the blank look in their eyes and know that inside their heads they are saying very quickly ABCDEFGHIJKL —and then start talking from there.

"Your lunch," I said, nodding at the clock behind his head.

He turned and looked, and then, as if caught pissing off the porch in daylight, turned back quickly.

"Never mind that!" he snapped.

"But you are taking up an inordinate amount of my time for no good purpose," he went on in that lecturing tone of voice. "I have been chosen to do a job, chosen to represent the people in this very important position, and your interruption is preventing me from carrying out my duties in a timely manner."

He went on, but I was getting hungry now. I had eaten scrambled eggs and toast at five o'clock in the morning and done a lot of work since then—the usual chores, getting a bath, although I knew I did not look clean now, driving up here in the gathering heat. My stomach was empty and about to get angry. As was Powers, who had advanced to that stage of his rhetoric.

"How dare you!" he said, leaning forward in his chair now, and about to shake his finger at me, I was sure. "People like you are a disgrace to this tribe. Look at you! You come in here half drunk, in a state of obvious dishevelment, demanding things that you have no right to and are beyond my ability to produce even if I wanted to!"

At this point I think he believed his own act. Spit bubbles had gathered in the left corner of his mouth.

I stood up, and I knew he believed he had won, but instead of going to the outside door, I took two quick steps around the corner of his desk, leaned over, and put my face mere inches from his.

"I want my check. Now." I used that normal tone of voice again, and I even smiled a little, and then I stood up but did not move away.

He shoved his chair back until it bounced off the bookshelves on the wall behind, swiveled it quickly, and lunged to his feet, running for the door as he shouted.

"Mary! Call the cops! Call the cops now!"

He fumbled at the door and ran out. I followed him, shut and locked the door behind him. Then I turned and looked at the room. He had seemed very nervous about what he was doing at that table. I walked over and looked. There was a ledger sheet on the table with a list of names on it and a dollar amount beside each ranging from $300 to $2,500, and beneath that sheet a separate sheet for each of the names on the first sheet. Each of the sheets with the individual names had a list of money figures on it. I checked the master sheet against the first named sheet. The dollar amount on the master matched the total of the figures on the individual sheet. There were two sets of these ledger sheets, and it appeared that the last entries on one set were not on the other. Probably, Johnson had been updating the second set by entering the last set of figures from the first sheets onto the second sheets. I took the first set, the one with the most recent entries, folded them in half, and put them in my purse. Then I went over to the desk, opened drawers.

Top one: too shallow to hold any large amount of checks, only pens, pencils, paper clips, and the like. Second drawer: a deep one, full of files. The top one on the right-hand side was also too narrow and the second deep one held a box of tissues, a bottle of Scotch, and a pair of pink panties, which I took out and laid on the desktop. I turned around the room, thinking. There was a cabinet right next to the front door, which someone was rattling now, demanding to be opened. Certainly not Johnson Powers. He would be afraid I might give him a black eye like the one he thought I had.

Someone in the outside office was yelling, "Then who DOES have the other key to this office?"

The cabinet door was locked. I got a letter opener out of the desk drawer, which also had a ring of keys, probably Johnson Powers's, placed the narrow end of the opener in the gap above the lock, and pried. The door came open with a pop. Inside were two deep wire baskets full of addressed and stamped envelopes. For a change, a tribal worker had done something efficient: the letters were piled in rows in alphabetical order. I found the one addressed to me and put it in my purse.

I walked over to the other door that led into the main hall. It was unlocked. I opened it and walked out. The people who had been standing in line were all trying to see into the little office in front of Johnson's, craning their necks and exclaiming. I turned left, walked down the corridor, out the back door, and around the building to the parking lot. My pickup seat was hot enough to burn my legs. I got out, got a gunny sack from behind the seat and put it over the hot spot, started the motor, and drove down to Big Bat's to get a chili cheese dog.

Just as I got my order, I saw all three tribal police cars drive by, sirens and lights going, heading toward the tribal offices. I sat in the little plastic booth by the window where I could see out as other people stared toward the offices and wondered what was going on.

I had finished the chili dog and was swallowing the last of my iced tea when one of the tribal police cars pulled into the parking lot. Bernie Bettelhouse got out on one side, hitching his pants up to their usual place beneath his big belly, laughing at something his skinny partner, Tim Galent, had said. They came in and ordered coffee and sat in the booth behind me.

"What was that at the tribal offices, Bernie?" I asked.

He shrugged. "Oh, just Johnson Powers whining about someone going to kill him over something or other."

"Why would anyone want to kill him?" I said.

"Why *wouldn't* anyone want to kill him is more like it," Tim said, and they both laughed.

In the pickup, I opened the envelope and looked at the check. It was the same amount it had been last time, and for the previous two years' worth of checks since the standard lease fees had been increased. I put it back, started the pickup, and started toward home.

On the way, I stopped at M&M Market in Jackson and bought more sugar, which I would need soon for making jelly, salt for making pickles, more jar flats—the rings could be reused if you were careful not to bend them when you opened the jar—and candy bars for the kids and for Clara Lately and me, too. We both had a sweet tooth as bad as the kids, but we would never let the kids know it. They might have suspected. I also got another big bottle of propane at the Farmer's Co-op. Running the range for canning takes a lot of propane.

The sun was still high when I got home, but Clara had finished whatever picking and canning she had wanted to do for the day and done a good job of cleaning up my kitchen range afterward. Canning makes such a mess because you cannot help but spill on the range top and then it burns on.

We sat outside and ate our candy bars, which had gone gooey in the heat but tasted just as good licked off the wrapper.

"Did everything go all right?" Clara asked tentatively. She over-indulged her eldest daughter and was naïve about religious and spiritual matters, but she was a good-hearted person who had a sense of propriety about private matters.

"Oh, very well, thank you," I said, but I did not elaborate. I gave Stella a little wink behind Clara's back.

After an hour, the last lid on the last jar that Clara had canned popped. The kids and I helped her put the jars in cardboard boxes and carry them out to her car. I thought she would want to put them in the trunk, but she insisted they should go in the back seat of her car, so we stacked them in as carefully as we could.

"If you stop too sudden you are going to have broken jars of green beans splattered on the inside of your windshield," I said.

"Oh, I'll be careful," she said.

When they had driven off down the lane to the main road, the kids hanging out the windows waving, Stella said to me, indignation in every line of her body, "Hazel, she had her trunk full of stuff she took out of the garden, even the biggest green tomatoes on the vines."

I laughed and hugged her.

"Well, I do not mind," I said. "She did us a big favor by coming over and staying here today. Come inside, and I will tell you what happened before we go do chores."

As I was drifting off to sleep, I thought that I needed to find a safe place to put those ledger sheets that Johnson Powers so obviously did not want me to see. The first name on the master sheet was George Wanbli.

9 Stella

No matter how many times over these many years I have had to put my birthdate down on official documents as August 4, I never do so without thinking privately that I was born in the month of ripening cherries. I don't remember all of them looking back, but I remember very well my birthday on August 4, 1963, the summer I turned thirteen. Hazel had planned not a party but a picnic and invited my best friend, Avril Lately, and his younger siblings, and his family was to meet us all at a little wide spot in the road that was halfway to He Dog Lake. The day fell on a Sunday, when, of course, Mr. Lately didn't have to work, and they had gone to early mass, so it was a perfect day for a family outing for all of us.

Hazel didn't say so, but I knew the picnic served a dual purpose: not only was it to celebrate my birthday, but it was also a good opportunity for Hazel and Avril's mother to pick the chokecherries that grew in abundance there, a wild fruit that was so tart as to be almost inedible fresh, but with plenty of sugar added, cooked down into tangy jelly. Avril and his father would most certainly get in some fishing, too, although most of their catch would probably be even more inedible than fresh chokecherries.

The lake usually yielded bass, crappie, perch, and bullheads, but this summer, the local fisherman reported catching only fish too small to keep and perch that they were surprised could still swim, as full of worms as they were.

It's odd, isn't it, what innocence we have when we plan something ordinary, and how much greater the shock seems to be when our plans go so very far awry. Hazel and I did the chores early. The night before, we had fried two chickens, not our own laying hens but ones bought at the grocery store in town, and that, along with fresh cucumbers, peppers, and tomatoes from the garden, and my cake, we packed into a big cardboard box carefully stowed in the front seat of the pickup between us.

It was still early when we drove down the lane to the main highway, a dew fallen so heavy that Hazel had to run the windshield wipers a swipe or two, the crow of a cock pheasant coming through the open windows. Halfway down the lane, a coyote, late in finishing up his night's foraging, ran across the road, dodging the headlights of the pickup. We drove east into the rising sun, Hazel pulling down the visor and still squinting to see. At Vidal, a town not even big enough to be called a wide place in the road, we stopped to wait for the Latelys, who had agreed to meet us there. Vidal has a post office attached to a little grocery store and two bars, Carson's and The Roundup, except everybody called them saloons, not bars, some outdated notion from a much earlier time perpetrated by John Wayne movies.

Carson's sat on the north side of the road just west of the grocery store, which did not have a name, while The Roundup was on the south side, the highway running between, and now and then a vehicle nearly ran over a drunk crossing the road to try the atmosphere and the drinks at the other bar. The grocery store owners and the bar owners had a neighborly arrangement: the grocery store didn't sell ice and the bars didn't sell soda pop—well, not in bulk, only one at a time to the underage partners and friends and kids of the hard drinkers.

The only time Hazel ever let me in a bar was to buy ice from Carson's when we went to He Dog, so on this day, I followed her across the sandy dirt in front of the bar and through the old blue wooden door. Inside was still cool, smelling of pine from the sawdust newly spread on the floor, and behind the bar a skinny old man sat reading a newspaper and listening to the Renfro Valley Gathering on the radio. The choir had just launched into "What a Friend We Have in Jesus" as we came in. He turned the radio down and asked could he help us, and Hazel told him we needed a couple of bags of ice. While they went to the side room of the bar to get it, I sat on a red leatherette-covered bar stool and spun it around and around, not real fast like little kids did, because I figured that as a teenager I should have more dignity, but a slower spin that I felt was perfectly appropriate for my age.

A soft burring noise came from the darker end of the room. I walked back to see, and there was a man in the booth. I hadn't seen him before because he was on the side of the booth that faced away from me, and sitting on the side where I didn't see him before because he wasn't sitting up but had his head down on the table, his mouth open as he snored and a fly buzzing around him, landing occasionally on his nose or his ear, or even his tongue, and he never noticed, never moved. Why must there always be a fly? How do flies know when a person is unable to swat them, or unaware of their presence? It was a big fly, one of those green-headed ones. I leaned closer, watching it, waiting to see if the man would wake up. His left hand, lying in a wet spill on the table, twitched a little. Part of the first joint of his first finger was missing, but a small bit of nail still grew on that finger, and the rest of his fingers had those thick yellow nails of men who have damaged their hands in one way or another many times in the course of hard labor.

He smelled sour, as if he had been drinking all night, vomited on himself, maybe worse. Beneath a worn, thin tan plaid shirt, the cowboy kind with the pointed yoke, I saw his back heaving up and down with each snoring breath. A new-looking white straw cowboy hat sat upside down on the cracked booth seat beside him; probably fell off when he passed out.

The fly crawled into his mouth, did not emerge, but the man kept snoring. I wondered if the fly might crawl back and come out his nose. I wondered how the fly could do that with the inside of the man's mouth and throat vibrating as he snored. I leaned over and peered into his mouth.

The fly came out with a buzz, right at my face; I let out a soft "ahhh" and jerked away, slapping at my face. The man came up out of the booth, his greasy salt-and-pepper hair standing up, his eyes slitted open, arms slapping back and forth in front of him several times as if he were swatting a swarm of flies. Then he stopped, half crouched, and looked around him, over his shoulders, side to side, in front, until his eyes settled on me, backing steadily away.

"I'm sorry, mister," I said. "I didn't mean to disturb you." I took a quick glance over my shoulder. I didn't see Hazel or the bar man, but I could hear them talking in the side room. As I was about to turn and run for it, the man snatched me by the wrist. Those yellow fingernails dug into my skin.

He yanked me close to him, his weepy red eyes inches from mine.

"Gurrrlll. You'd better watch out, gurrlll. He is coming."

He stank like vomit, like shit, like carrion. He drew his other arm back, way back behind him, as if preparing to slap me, and then he dropped my hand, flung himself in a circle, shouting, "He's coming! He's coming!" and he whirled around and around the room, his worn-out boots kicking up the sawdust.

"He's coming for you! You'll see! He's coming for you!"

The bar man came out of the back room with Hazel at his heels, and from around behind the bar, a fluffy, three-legged white dog yapping at the bar man.

"Beale! Beale! Pipe down or I'll throw you out!" the bar man yelled, and just as he did, the drunken man fell to his knees and rolled over as if felled by a baseball bat, but no one had touched him.

The little white dog hop-ran to the man and stood over him, its one front leg propped on the man's chest, snarling at the bar man.

Hazel grabbed me and pulled me away.

"What's going on here?" she demanded.

"That man was asleep, and then he woke up and started yelling," I said.

She glanced at me suspiciously, but the bar man spoke up just then.

"It's just Beale," he said. "He's a little crazy after he's been drinking all night, but he's harmless enough, so I let him sleep it off in that back booth. Lord knows he was in no shape to drive home. It was the Christian thing to do. That's his dog."

Hazel said, "He doesn't look like he would bite, but that dog might."

The bar man shrugged and tried to coax the dog away, but he only snarled and curled up beside the fallen Beale.

"He's very protective. He was a stray run over crossing the street in Jackson. The driver went on, but Beale took the dog to the vet. Couldn't save the dog's leg, but saved the dog. He's very protective."

Hazel squeezed my shoulder.

"Wait outside in the pickup, honey. I'll just be a minute getting the ice."

I had just stepped outside the door when the Latelys' car came up the road, stopping in front of the grocery store and letting the kids out of the back seat while Mrs. Lately rolled out of the passenger side.

"Avril," I said before he said anything. "There's a crazy drunk in the bar. He was threatening me!"

"What?" His eyes were disbelieving. "Why would any old drunk threaten you?"

His brothers, Melvin and Norris and Lester, came pelting up behind him.

"What drunk threatened Stella?" Melvin asked.

"Stella says some drunk threatened her," Avril answered.

"He did! Somebody named Beale in Carson's when Hazel and I went in there to get ice."

"What did he say?" Avril asked.

"He grabbed my wrist and wouldn't let go, and he said 'He's coming!' He just kept saying that, and then he let go and went whirling around in circles until he fell down."

Avril clucked his tongue.

"Oh, you're making a big deal out of nothing. He sounds like a dumb old drunk is all."

Mrs. Lately hollered at the kids, "Come pick out what kind of soda you want or you'll have to take whatever I pick."

The three younger boys ran off, but Avril said, "Now that you're a teenager, you start making a big deal out of everything, just like Nancy does." Avril and I were in the same grade in school, but his birthday wasn't until October.

I slugged him in the arm to prove I was not too good for him.

"I'm not Nancy," I said.

Avril looked me up and down.

"No, you're not," he said, grinning. "She has boobs."

When everyone had gotten ice and pop and put the two together in ice chests and loaded them, the Latelys extra carefully because their ice chest went in the trunk with the fishing poles, we headed east, a two vehicle convoy toward the lake.

Hazel did not mention Beale, the drunk in the bar, to me or to the Latelys, and there was no chance to ask her because I rode in the car with the Latelys while Mrs. Lately rode with Hazel.

I always knew exactly where to turn off to He Dog Lake because just before the turnoff, there is a small house on the south side of the road painted a coral pink. No one around the rez or in the towns painted their houses anything but white; no one got any more adventurous than to paint around the window with green instead of blue for trim, except whoever painted this pink house. I guess somebody must have known who had done so, but no one I knew ever said so, and no one at all had lived in the house for years. We called that house Nellie's Nightie, and the kids would watch for it and yell, "There's Nellie's Nightie; next turn to He Dog!"

The road was a single lane, a pair of deep ruts in high grass pasture that wiped the underside of low vehicles as they were driven over it, and passed through three gates, which the kids had to open and close for the cars to pass. The lake was small, but seemed bigger as it was long and shaped like a sea horse seen from the side. In most years the sandy banks rose steeply some ten feet above the water, but that year had been a very wet one, so fishermen could sit on the bank and dangle their feet in the water—*could* do it, but most would not for fear of scaring the fish away.

Mr. Lately and the three younger boys got out their fishing gear immediately, Mr. Lately putting the hooks on the lines while the boys ran through the high grass scaring up grasshoppers to catch for bait. Hazel and Mrs. Lately set off scouting through the widely spaced trees some hundred yards from the bank.

"I remember last year, there was a pair of chokecherry trees a little down this way," Hazel said. "The cherries should be about ripe now, unless someone has been here ahead of us and picked them all."

Avril and I followed along for a while but turned off on a cow path that led off to the west through thicker stands of trees and undergrowth. Farther over in the woods, there was a limestone outcropping and, mostly hidden by thorny brush, a little cave underneath, just deep enough to shelter a couple of people, if they were small people, against rain. We had discovered it a couple of years earlier when the Latelys' dog had run off after a rabbit and we had followed it to this cave. The dog had run off from the Latelys' place to somewhere else a few months later, but the cave remained, a place that Avril and I kept secret from his brothers and everybody else, too.

It took a bit of work to find the place again; the heavy rains had brought on a big crop of underbrush that disguised the way to the cave as well the entrance. We were thoroughly scratched with briars when we found it, pulled aside the obstructing branches, and crawled in, hot and sweaty. A limestone cave, the interior was light, about four feet deep and the same high, but the roof slanted slightly from front to back so there wasn't a straight-up part to rest your back against. I suppose water running through the hill for years and years had dissolved the limestone and left this little space. There might be other caves, were almost certainly other hollow spaces within the hill, but without openings to the outside, we would never know of them.

Right above the entrance to the cave on the inside is a lip, a sill about six inches wide where some years ago, Avril and I had put a flip-top tobacco can with a note in it. It read:

To whoever finds this. We use this cave, too. Who are you?

No one had ever written their names on the paper and left it for us to find, maybe because we hadn't left the pencil, and besides, who carries a spare pencil around with them to leave notes to strangers? But Avril and I believed that no one had written an answer on the note because no one else but us knew about the cave, which made it all the more special to us and all the more reason to keep it a secret from everybody else.

We crawled inside, turned around in the cramped space to face the entrance, and checked the tobacco box for the note.

Our note was still there, the penciled message fading a little, but there was no response.

"You think we will ever get an answer to the message?" Avril asked.

"Not unless rabbits learn to write," I said.

He put the box back above the cave opening, and we sat for a moment looking out through the green brambles.

"I'm sorry I made fun of you about the drunk," he said.

I didn't answer, and then he said, "I guess it was really scary."

"Yeah," I said. "Not just scary, creepy."

"What's he say, again?"

I told him the whole story, what the man said, what he looked like. Avril shook his head but could offer no meaning for what the man had said.

"You were probably right the first time," I said. "It doesn't mean anything. He was just some goofy old drunk." But as much as I wanted to believe my own words, I still felt there was some deep knowledge in that stinking man's red eyes about some yet-to-be-fulfilled awful event.

He reached into his pocket and brought out a little white box and handed it to me.

"I saw you looking at this in Jackson. Here."

It was a birthstone pendant on a dainty chain, not expensive, but something I knew Avril had to save his allowance to buy for me. I was touched.

"Avril, this is really nice of you. Thank you," I said. His face had turned red; he turned away and dug at the side of the cave with a stick. I could tell he was afraid I might get the wrong idea, but that he had been willing to take the chance to give me something he knew I really wanted.

We were both wearing jeans and white tee shirts and old black basketball shoes, the summer uniform for all of us kids, except I had an orange hat, one that came from the feed mill in Jackson four years ago, a kid's size. The feed mill had only given them out for kids that one year. Avril hadn't gotten one, but he always admired mine. We were at the one brief moment in our youth when boys and girls were much the same size from head to toe. I took off the cap and said, "Here, trade you."

His round berry eyes went rounder. "Naah, I can't let you do that."

"Look, I wanted the necklace worse. Besides, like you said, I'm a teenager now, so I probably should act more like a girl." I held out the cap. "Here, I mean it. I want you to have it."

We went back to the cars, an easier passage now that we had pressed down and pressed aside the brush and brambles. Melvin came running up with a string of three little bass to show us, none of them longer than five inches. When cleaned with head and tail removed, each of them would not amount to a mouthful, but he was excited, and so Avril and I tried to be excited for him.

At the picnic spot, Mr. Lately had dug a shallow hole in the ground, surrounded it with rocks, and lit a few dry branches aflame. He had brought an old steel refrigerator rack to place over the fire for grilling any fish they caught, although there were no other fish but Melvin's.

Hazel and Mrs. Lately were setting out food on an old blanket spread beneath a tree, Mrs. Lately puffing and groaning as she leaned her little round body this way and that.

"Did you find chokecherries?" I asked.

"We did!" Hazel said. "And no one else has been here before us unless you count some birds."

I thought of the smooth chokecherry jelly we would have soon, and more to store for winter, the best sweet in the world on top of buckwheat pancakes with butter on a cold winter day—or even a hot summer one, but the jelly always ran out before the winter did.

We ate then, the fried chicken and fresh vegetables that Hazel and I had brought, the baked beans and potato salad that was Mrs. Lately's contribution, and when we had finished, Hazel asked if I wanted to cut my birthday cake, but I said, no, I wanted to wait a while, I was too full, even though Melvin and Norris and Lester gave me dirty looks.

When the paper plates and cups were collected for the trash sack, the food wrapped and put away, I felt sleepy, so while Hazel and Mrs. Lately sat on the blanket chatting, I stretched out on the back seat of the Latelys' car with both back doors open so the breeze could come through. When I woke up a couple of hours later, everyone was gone.

The milk pails that Hazel had brought for picking chokecherries were gone and so were the two women. From down at the edge of the lake, I heard the boys quarreling among themselves and Mr. Lately's voice furiously telling them to shut up, they were scaring the fish, so I walked down that way.

Melvin and Norris and Lester sat in a row, their lower lips poked out sullenly, elbowing each other.

"Where's Avril?" I whispered to Mr. Lately.

He looked around, over both shoulders, up and down the bank, shrugged.

"Well, I thought he was here," he said, very low.

"He said he was going to look for forked branches to make slingshots and he wouldn't let us go," Melvin said.

"Oh," I said and started back toward the car and beyond to the woods and the path to the cave.

"Can I come, too?" shouted Melvin, but I didn't have to answer because I heard a loud slap and a howl, and Mr. Lately say, "I *told* you to be quiet!"

Avril was not at the cave, or anyplace along the path to the cave, so I walked on through the woods to the trees where Hazel and Mrs. Lately were picking chokecherries. The trees are not big; even the older ones rarely get more than twenty feet high.

They had picked all the chokecherries off the lower branches, and Hazel held the tree bent over so Mrs. Lately could pick the ones that couldn't be reached otherwise.

"You seen Avril?" I asked.

"No," Mrs. Lately said, "but he wandered through here, oh, I guess an hour or so ago."

"Which way was he headed?" I asked.

She gestured vaguely to the south, away from the car and the cave in the opposite direction. I walked on through the trees. The farther I walked, the thicker the underbrush and trees growing on a steep bank with no real path through them. Finally, I gave up trying to parallel the lake bank, climbed through the trees and brush to the hill a quarter of a mile away to the west, and stood there looking down over the lake, rippling now in the afternoon breeze. I could see the car and Hazel's pickup parked in the treeless space, and a little of the light-colored blanket beneath the tree where we had eaten our lunch. I could see Melvin—or maybe it was Norris or Lester—pop up from the creek bank and run around in the brush a hundred yards beyond the car. I supposed Mr. Lately had put them to catching more grasshoppers for bait. I couldn't see Hazel or Mrs. Lately, but I knew that they had probably finished picking the fruit on the two trees they had found and were looking for others. I had seen a couple a little ways past the two they had found first.

Across the lake on the east side and half a mile or so farther south, I saw a couple of vehicles parked, other people taking advantage of this fine summer day to fish or picnic or whatever. I looked west and saw the prairie grasses, now starting to go yellow with the dryer end of the summer coming on. The land rolled a bit, cut through here and there with little ditches and bigger gullies, some of them big enough to hide a tall person, but I did not see Avril's orange capped head. I didn't think he would have gone off for hours without coming back to see if I wanted to go wherever it was he was going.

"Avril! Avril!" I shouted, and turning, shouted his name again and again, but he did not answer. I walked along the hill ridge back toward the car, calling again from time to time, and when I came up on the road we had followed down to the lake, I followed it, looking for his tracks in the sandy ruts, but saw nothing. He would not have gotten into the lake to swim across, I was sure of it. Avril liked splashing around in water, but he didn't like swimming, didn't like getting his face in the water, but I was probably the only one of his friends who knew that because he knew I wouldn't tell anyone or call him sissy.

Something bad had happened. I thought about Beale in the saloon as I ran down the road to tell the Latelys and Hazel. Something bad had happened.

10 Stella

Now that I am an adult, I have often wondered about something that I first experienced that summer day I turned thirteen. Why do people who are seemingly intelligent and quick thinking, when faced with a person shouting out an emergency, suddenly become stupid, dull witted, insensible fools who have lost their sense of hearing? Yes, they become temporarily deaf. A person in desperate need runs up to a group of people, shouts out an emergency, and every one of that group without exception jerks upright, eyes wide, staring from side to side as if Jesus Christ or Mohammed or Buddha or Tunkasila will suddenly appear from left or right and make everything all right. They hear the nature of the emergency, and yet they do not react sensibly with any organization of thought, word, or deed. Indeed, their first response is to acknowledge that they have gone deaf. They say, "Huh?"

The messenger repeats the emergency, the crowd shifts from foot to foot, exchanges glances with other group members while avoiding the eyes of the messenger. Then the crowd regains part of their hearing, and they utter the questions that journalism students are told they should answer in any news story: Who, What, When, Where, How, and Why. The answers to most of these questions will have nothing to do with the emergency (for example: a car going ninety miles an hour goes off a cliff into a river and the people inside will drown if they are not pulled out very soon, but the crowd doesn't immediately call the rescue people, get ropes, etc., oh no. The crowd hears about the car going off the cliff and they ask, "How did that happen?" "When?" and so on, none of which questions matter at the moment, only rescuing the people in distress. The questions can be asked *later*), and will not contribute to solving the emergency, and yet every member of the crowd not only asks these questions but rarely listens to the answers, even if the messenger has the time, knowledge, and inclination to respond. Most members of the crowd respond to the six journalism answers by going deaf again: "Huh?"

Some members of the crowd will react by screaming, sometimes repeatedly. I wonder how their branch of the human ancestral tree had survived. These humans' prehistoric ancestors should have been eaten by the saber-toothed tigers that attacked them, while they jumped up and down and screamed instead of having sense enough to *run like hell*, but obviously, those screamers survived to reproduce, because their descendants are everywhere. I can only surmise that saber-toothed tigers and other large predators despised screaming as much as I do, and that instead of attacking the screamers, the tigers ran like hell to escape that horrible, ear-piercing sound, which might explain why there are so many screamers around today, and also why so many nonscreamers go temporarily deaf in emergencies.

I learned this on my thirteenth birthday when Avril disappeared, and in all the years since, the original lesson has not been negated, only reinforced.

The longer I stood on that ridge above the west end of He Dog Lake looking intently over everything I could see, shouting for Avril who did not respond, the more convinced I became that Beale's prediction had come true. "He" had come for me, but found Avril wearing my orange cap instead.

I ran down the hill, first to Mr. Lately, still sitting on the bank, fishing line slack in the water, Melvin, Norris, and Lester still sitting in that sullen, mostly silent row beside him. They turned as one when they heard me pelting up behind, Mr. Lately, I'm sure, to tell me to be quiet, I was scaring the fish. None of them said a word, only stared at me with big eyes and mouths partly opened, and I was breathing so hard and clutching the stitch in my side that I couldn't speak for a couple of minutes. Just as I saw Mr. Lately's face change from that stupid, slow-witted dumbfoundedness to anger—preparing to yell at me for making noise, I raised my hand to forestall it, and got out a few words.

"Avril," I gasped. "Avril is gone."

"Huh?" From Mr. Lately. No words from the boys.

"Avril is gone," I repeated.

"Gone? Gone where?" Mr. Lately asked. The boys had closed their mouths and were looking from left to right, and I give them some credit. Maybe they were looking for Avril, not for Jesus, Mohammed, Shiva, or Tunkasila to save them.

"I don't know," I said. "He left right after lunch, and I can't find him anywhere."

Mr. Lately looked down at his hands for a moment. "Well, maybe his mother knows where he is. Did you ask her?"

"Not yet. But I saw her and Hazel earlier when I first started looking for him, and they said he had passed them walking south down the lake bank. But I went that way and farther than he would have gone and back up the hill and around, looking for him and hollering for him, and he's gone. I can't find him."

Mr. Lately clambered to his feet, for once ignoring his fishing line.

"Avril's gone? Gone where?" he repeated.

"I don't know. I need help finding him," I said.

Melvin and Norris and Lester exchanged glances again. Melvin said, "Let's go tell Mom!" and they jumped up and ran for the car and the tree with the picnic blanket beneath it.

Mr. Lately looked from side to side.

"Well, let me reel in my line, and I'll help. He can't have gone very far."

I followed the boys to the picnic tree, where Hazel and Mrs. Lately had been napping on the blanket but now were half sitting and leaning on their elbows, blinking. All three boys at once were trying to tell them about Avril gone missing.

I butted in and talked loud over their excited blue-jay chattering.

"Avril is missing," I said. "He's gone, and I went the direction you said he went, but I didn't find him. He doesn't answer when I holler for him. He's gone."

I have to give Hazel credit. She's neither a screamer nor deaf, and not stupid and insensible, but she doesn't move as fast as I wish she would either. She stood up slowly and didn't say anything.

Mrs. Lately gasped, "Avril is *g-o-n-e?*" The pitch of her voice rose with each syllable she uttered, and then the screaming began and she rolled over on her side on the blanket, which did nothing to muffle sound. Melvin and Norris and Lester clapped hands over their ears and ran toward their dad, coming up from the lake now, one slogging step at a time, his fishing pole over his shoulder, a piece of weed caught on the bobber swinging behind him.

I expected Hazel to slap Mrs. Lately like people do in books and movies, but she didn't. She very deliberately put her foot—and Hazel had quite large feet—on Mrs. Lately's small hand lying on the blanket. Mrs. Lately took no notion at first, but Hazel slowly put more and more of her weight on Mrs. Lately's hand. The intensity of the screams diminished a little as Mrs. Lately tried unsuccessfully to jerk her hand from beneath Hazel's foot, while Hazel stared expressionless at me. Hazel leaned onto that foot, and Mrs. Lately's screams turned into words:

"AHRRRRR! You're—AHHRROWWWW—You're standing—You're STANDING ON MY HAND!"

Hazel jumped back then, and Mrs. Lately sat up, snatched her hand to her chest, and sat rocking, alternately moaning oHHH, but the screaming had stopped.

Hazel quickly sat by Mrs. Lately.

"Oh, my dear friend, I am so clumsy; you know, I wouldn't hurt you for the world. Here, let me see—" she said, and interspersed her comforting with questions of me: "Where and when did you see him last—no, no, it isn't broken, only a little, shall I say, *pinched*—did you find anything he might have dropped anywhere?—here, let me get some of the ice water from the cooler, it'll take the pain away—"

And while she wet a cloth in the melted ice water in the cooler, she asked more questions of me, but when I had answered she did not immediately set out to do anything, but only sat beside Mrs. Lately with the cold cloth on her hand.

Mr. Lately propped his fishing pole against the tree, stood there with his hands on his hips watching his wife. The boys were hopping up and down and jabbering.

"Dad, Dad, let's go look for him, huh?" and "Yeah, Dad. Suppose he fell in the lake and drowned? We might not find his body for weeks and then it would be all icky and slimy and stinky."

At this last Mrs. Lately started and looked like she was about to get her screamer tuned up again, but Hazel tilted the glass of tea she held into Mrs. Lately's mouth. She had to swallow fast or choke.

I wanted action, immediate action.

"Mr. Lately," I said. "Maybe we should go look for him. I know the last place anybody saw him was at the chokecherry trees down that way."

"Yeah, yeah, Dad!" Norris said.

"We could all spread out and look down that—" I went on, but Hazel interrupted.

"No," she said, quietly but firmly. "If we all go running around in the woods and up and down the lake, something not good is likely to happen. Someone is going to trip over a branch and sprain an ankle, or fall in the lake or worse. Here is what we are going to do."

That's all I wanted: someone to make sense, someone to organize things in a useful way, and of course, I should have known it would be Hazel, but I did not like the plan she came up with.

"Clara, you take the kids and drive to the Rosebud Tribal Police station—you know where that is—and get them to send some people out to help search. Then you and the kids stay there; if anyone comes in with any information, you will be the first to know. Mr. Lately and I will stay here and look down the lake bank both ways and up to the ridge, and get any other fisherman out here—I saw a couple of pickup trucks across the lake earlier—to help search. Now, we need to get all our stuff loaded back in the cars so that is out of the way."

I knew what Hazel was doing, and I didn't like it. The part about getting stuff loaded wasn't necessary; but it was so like the way Hazel managed me at home: when people might resist doing something she wanted them to do, she put them to work so they couldn't think as easily, couldn't think up a good reason not to do whatever it was she wanted them to do. And I didn't like being sent off with Mrs. Lately and the little kids to the tribal police. Well, I didn't mind going to tell the tribal police, but I didn't want to stay there! That was another of Hazel's favorite ploys—send the people who might be hard to manage off on an errand and think up another errand to keep them away until you had done what you needed to do.

"No! No, I will not be sent off!" I yelled. "Avril is my friend, my very best friend, and I want to help look for him."

"Stella. Honey—"

"No!" I stomped my foot; I dared that far, a defiant action that I had long since been disciplined out of doing. "I am not a child, not a child!"

"Listen to me now," Hazel said, and she pulled me by the arm away into the trees, through briars clawing at my pants legs, a lot farther away than was strictly necessary to keep the Latelys from hearing what she had to say to me that I most emphatically did *not* want to hear.

We stopped beneath an old lightning-struck cottonwood tree, and she let go my arm and turned her back to the Latelys. I was suddenly aware that I had run hard and long in the heat and that the metallic stench of sweat clung to me, but she did not comment.

"Look at them," she commanded. "Carefully, not staring."

I did, at Mrs. Lately, a ball of misery on the worn old pink blanket, clutching her hand and moaning, but not screaming; at Mr. Lately standing off the edge of the blanket looking at her, then left, then right, as if hoping that Avril would suddenly appear and all this would be over; at Marvin and Norris and Lester, capering like a trio of wild goats, sing-songing "Avril's gone, Avril's gone" like idiots.

"Somebody has to take charge of this pack of fools." She caught herself. "Well, they are not exactly fools; I know they are upset as anyone should be—but never mind, somebody has to take charge and none of them are capable. One of us has to stay here and get Mr. Lately to be methodical and useful in looking for Avril. And one of us has to go with Mrs. Lately to the tribal police and tell them what happened in terms they can understand and then keep her out of the way so the cops and Mr. Lately and whatever other adults we can recruit can organize a sensible search."

I nodded.

"Now, which of us do you think can best get Mr. Lately and possibly other people to help look?"

I didn't want to answer because I knew the answer and it wasn't the one I wanted to admit.

"Once Mrs. Lately is away from here, she can be distracted, and

the kids will give her something else to think about. But you—"
I noted she said *you*, meaning me, and I didn't like that either,
but I shut up and listened.

"—you can keep her distracted and talk her out of any other
dumb ideas she might come up with that would be less than useful." She stopped then and waited for me to say something.

"What do you think happened to him?" I asked, scratching at
a mosquito bite, one of many that I knew I would notice soon,
bites from the mosquitoes that swarmed along the edge of the
lake farther south where a creek used to drain into the lake but
had now, deep into the summer, begun to dry up, leaving a scum-
my green puddle perfect for mosquito breeding.

"He could have fallen down and hit his head and be unconscious
somewhere out in these woods. Or maybe he just went off somewhere and fell asleep like the rest of us did after dinner and is so
sound asleep he did not hear you call. It is impossible to know."
There was something in the expression of her eyes that said she
might have an idea, but she was not willing to tell me yet.

"You are only thirteen years old," she went on. "I know I'm
asking you as a kid to do an adult job, when Mrs. Lately is the
adult who should be taking care of you, but this is how it is, and
it is probably always going to be this way. For the rest of your
life, beginning now, you will have to be the responsible one when
anything bad happens. I know the truth is not a good birthday
present."

I thought that she was manipulating me with the first part,
about needing to be the grown-up in this situation, but I believed
her deeply about the last part. I believed that she was speaking
from her own experience, telling me that in every group of people there is one person, no matter how young or how old, who
has to take charge, to be capable, to keep the other people from
running stark-raving mad and doing something completely ir-
rational. Those people are the ones who make good policemen

or firemen—I know that now, years later, and I also know that when the people in charge of all the things in the world, the presidents and heads of corporations, run everything into chaos, it is usually those one or two persons, who have names no one ever knows, who keep the world tottering along on the brink instead of crashing over.

I accepted her call, and I said, "Yes."

"Good." She squeezed my arm again and turned without another word.

Fifteen minutes later everything except for some bottles of soda left in the ice chest and the water jug had been loaded into the Latelys' car. Mrs. Lately, much calmed, was in the driver's seat with me riding shot-gun and the boys in the back, quiet now that Hazel had talked to each one quietly and alone, as she had done with me.

It must have been about four o'clock in the afternoon when Mrs. Lately drove up the long, sloping hill to the ridge, turned south, and drove slowly over the twin ruts to the first gate. The boys and I looked out the windows watching and looking for anything that might be Avril, but we saw nothing. In another five hours, with the sun gone down, it would be impossible to search.

Mrs. Lately concentrated on driving, her hands clutching the steering wheel as if it were a lifeline, moving one hand quickly to shift gears when we had to stop for each gate. I opened them, waited until she had driven through, and fastened them shut again, feeling that shutting them was the least important thing to do but doing it anyway because the custom in this country is that if you open a gate, you shut the gate, because people graze their livestock in these pastures; those livestock are their livelihood, and you don't leave gates open so those animals can stray.

It seemed to take forever to get back to the highway where we could go faster, but in fact, it was probably less than half an hour, and I hoped, oh, I hoped, that Hazel and Mr. Lately would have already found Avril, and we would all have a good laugh when we got back, and Avril would be embarrassed, and I would thump him good.

The Rosebud Tribal Police Station and Jail is small, but always open and busy on a Sunday because relatives come in to pick up any of their kin that got in trouble on the Saturday night before and thrown in jail. So, there were four people standing in front of the counter filling out paperwork and talking to the three tribal cops, and several other people—mothers, fathers, siblings, cousins—sitting in chairs waiting, or running around the office, or standing outside on the wide porch smoking cigarettes and looking bored.

Mrs. Lately got in line behind a tall woman wearing a green coat, a coat too heavy and warm for midsummer, a woman who looked very angry at whoever she had come to spring from the jail. I didn't let her stand there, but said, "Excuse us, we have an emergency," to the green coat back and stepped up to the counter.

A skinny little cop with big glasses stood there filling out paperwork. I thought he looked like Jiminy Cricket. He didn't look up. Mrs. Lately waited. I didn't.

"Sir," I said. "We have an emergency."

He still didn't look up. "Everyone has an emergency," he said.

Mrs. Lately sighed, but she was twitchy, stepping from foot to foot like she had to go to the bathroom, slumping down, standing up straight again, switching her handbag from one arm to the other with a jerky motion.

"sir," I repeated. "This is Mrs. Lately. Her family and mine were fishing over at He Dog and her son Avril is missing. Gone. We looked for him and can't find him."

Jiminy Cricket finished the page he was writing on and looked up at me over his glasses, glanced at Mrs. Lately, and back at me.

"Who are you?" he asked.

"I'm Hazel Latour's granddaughter, Stella, from over on Pine Ridge."

He tapped the pen against his chin, a chin that was deeply pitted and pockmarked.

"Latour. You're the people with that *wakan* turkey."

"Yeah, yeah," I said. I didn't want to get trapped in a time-consuming conversation about the white turkey. "But sir, we need some cops—some policemen—to come help us find Avril Lately."

He turned the page on the report he was writing, started filling out the next page. I looked at the other two cops; the bigger, fatter one was also filling out paperwork and asking questions of the old man who stood at the counter. Just as I drew a deep breath to start screaming—sometimes being loud, obnoxious, and insensible is a useful tactic—one of the other cops, the skinnier of the two other cops, an older man with big, blotchy stains on the front of his uniform, turned around from talking to a youngish woman.

He looked at me and said, "Well, another lost kid up at He Dog, huh?"

I closed my mouth. "Yes sir."

He had a wad of gum in his mouth that he rotated from one side to the other. Without turning his head, he yelled, "ALFRED!" and waited a minute, yelled again, "ALFRED!"

A fourth cop, younger and bigger than either of the others, came running from a door in the back, a ring of keys jingling in his hand.

"Yeah, yeah. I can't be everywhere at once. What do you want?"

"How many men we got still back there in jail? Sober and walking around, I mean."

The young cop looked off into space a minute. "Four. No, I miscount. Five."

The woman in the green coat behind me snapped out, "Four. I'm taking my son home. He's not going to spend half the night running around He Dog Lake hunting for some kid."

Mrs. Lately lifted the arm with the handbag on it as if to take a roundhouse swing at the woman behind her. I caught her arm and said, "Wait!"

The older cop said, "All right. Those four just got their fines eliminated if they'll be part of a search party for this kid—what's his name?"

"Avril Lately," Mrs. Lately said.

"April," the cop said.

"AVRIL," Mrs. Lately snapped.

The cop didn't answer as he glanced at the clock.

"It's close on five o'clock. We got about three hours, maybe three and a half before dark. Get those guys loaded in the number six cruiser and get out there."

"What if they would rather pay their fine?" the young cop asked.

"They won't." the older cop said.

"What side of the lake?" the older cop asked me.

"West side, down where that little bit of land points out in the lake."

"There a big old cottonwood there close to the edge of the lake? And another lightning-stuck one a little ways away?"

"Yeah, that's where we had lunch. That's where Avril wandered away from."

"Hear that?" the older cop asked. "And be sure to check in at Winchells' place, and that trailer of their hired hand. Also Bert Ellis's place. Anybody else's place you can think of. Kid could have wandered in any of those places."

"Got it," the younger cop answered, took the keys and hurried back through the far door.

Jiminy Cricket pointed his pen at me. "You still got that turkey?"

"Yeah," I said. I pulled Mrs. Lately by the coat sleeve over to the line of chairs. The boys wandered over to a soda machine and started poking at it.

One of the worst jobs in the world is waiting, just waiting. After I grew up, I had this friend of mine once who always said he wanted a job where he didn't have to do anything but sit there. No walking, no lifting, no talking, no writing, no nothing. Just sit there. So he thought he found the perfect job as a guard at the Wyoming State Prison in Rawlins. He lasted less than a month. He said he had discovered that the hardest work in the world is to sit still and wait. I knew that when I was thirteen years old.

We waited. Melvin and Norris and Lester cadged some change from Mrs. Lately for the soda machine and then got in a fight over the one bottle of orange Nehi left in the machine. She took it away from them and poured it down the sink in the bathroom, sent them outside to play with the kids of other people waiting too, for I don't know what or who. Maybe for the four men that had been deputized to search for Avril.

The third sweep hand on the clock went around, but I don't think it bore any relationship to the other two hands, which did not seem to move at all until I had looked away for a while, and when I looked back, they had each moved such a tiny, tiny bit. I wondered if Avril was somewhere, awake, aware, but unable to make anyone hear him, and if time had slowed to a molasses-in-winter crawl for him as well. Mrs. Lately had nothing to say, nothing at all, so there was nothing for me to prevent her from doing. She, too, waited.

I scrunched myself into a ball in the chair, pulling up my feet and leaning my head on the chair arm.

Television came to our neck of the woods when I was about ten years old, an event that I remember very well because Linda Steiner was in the fifth grade with me. Her parents were the richest family around, something that Linda liked everyone else to be aware of, so of course, we all heard a month in advance of the event that the Steiners were getting television. Most of the men were interested in the fact, too, because men like gadgets and this was a very new, expensive gadget. I heard them talk about it around their cribbage board at the post office when Hazel sent me in to collect the mail. They discussed which channels they thought the Steiners could pull in, even though there were only two within any possible range of reception, or so I heard them say, but they were convinced that if the antenna were mounted on a pole at least fifty feet high, the Steiners could pull in both the Rapid City station and another one from some far-away town I'd never heard of before: Reliance.

On the night that Mr. Steiner finally unboxed his television and hooked it up, half the neighborhood was there to witness the event, especially the men, who wanted to help or at least give advice. I didn't see it, only heard about it later, because Hazel wouldn't go or let me go. She said that if television caught on and surpassed radio then she might be interested, but she wasn't about to have her nose poked under someone else's dress for any reason, and wouldn't allow me to shame myself so either.

She did let me go with the other kids from school one evening when Linda invited us all to come over and watch some show called *Lassie*. It was supposed to be about a boy and his dog, a kind of miracle dog that saved the boy from all kinds of bad things. I couldn't follow much of it, though, because to me the television looked like blurry figures moving through a snow storm, and the other kids were so busy talking (Linda kept telling them all to shut up) that I didn't hear what people on the show were supposed to be saying. I did understand enough to tell Hazel what it was about: the boy got lost, fell down a well, I think, and Lassie led people to the well, barking until they figured out she wanted them to follow her.

Hazel said that dogs were nice to have around, friendly and all that, and there might be a dog that was smart enough to save people, but she didn't know any personally. That's when I first heard the expression about not believing everything you see on television, but then, with all that blurry stuff, I really hadn't seen much. But I suppose that notion of a not-so-smart animal saving a lost and endangered boy made an impression on me.

I sat on the porch in the full sun of a bright spring morning, that perfect time when the rays are not too hot, but warm you deeply, planting the memory of that heat to draw upon when the wind comes out of the north and the slanting pale sun serves only to draw blue shadows across the snow. I held a pan full of cracked corn on my lap, throwing a handful from time to time to a white turkey. Presently, several chickens came running, joining the turkey. There were black-and-white-speckled Plymouth Rocks hens mixed with some Domaneckers and one big black rooster, jostling and pushing each other and the wild pheasants every time I pitched a fresh handful of corn from the pan. The chickens moved closer to me; the pan was almost empty, so I pitched smaller amounts, which only brought the chickens, especially the black rooster, closer to me, demanding in loud clucking voices and growing larger and larger, as big as an ostrich. I looked at the door behind me, the door to the house, but it was closed, and then the rooster pushed me off the porch.

I sprawled sideways; the rooster stood over me, opened his mouth, and a fly came out, and the fly said, "He is coming! He is coming!" Then he flew in circles around my head, pulling me into the air and towing me from the porch, around the corner of the house, into shade that got darker and darker, and the turkey cried out behind me, and the hens chattered, but I could not stop myself. I still held the pan with a few handfuls of corn left, and as I was towed, I dribbled the broken kernels a few at a time as I was pulled along, toward this bank behind the house with a cave opening where I was pulled inside and flung to the floor. The rooster left then, but the cave was not the small, light one at He Dog Lake; no, this one went deep behind me, dark, and a cold, fetid air wafted past my face. I tried to sit up, but I was wrapped with wiry lengths of brambles that dug into my wrists and ankles, piercing even the tough denim of my jeans.

Then, as if I were separated from myself and floating far above the earth, I saw the white turkey back at the house, saw her run to the door and peck at it, pecking louder and louder until the pecking sounded like a woodpecker with a big hammer, and finally, the door opened and Hazel came out. The turkey gobbled at her, ran down the steps, ran back to her. She spoke to the turkey, a questioning tone. The turkey turned its head to the side, blinked its eyes, went down the steps again and ate the first half kernel of corn that I had dropped. Hazel followed the turkey, who followed the trail of cracked corn around the corner, slowly, and then the turkey stopped pecking and eating the corn and began to run, and I returned to my body in the cave, felt the turkey pecking at my bramble wire bindings, and Hazel released me and the cave turned pink, walls flowing in and out, in and out, like silk blowing in a breeze, like a fancy nightgown.

I screamed, "It's Nellie's Nightie!"

The turkey gobbled and pulled at my clothes.

Mrs. Lately said, "Wake up, Stella. You're having a bad dream." She had my sleeve in her hand, tugging me back and forth.

"It's Avril," I said. "Avril is at Nellie's Nightie!"

"Huh?" she said.

11 Hazel

I wish I had never stolen those ledger sheets from Johnson Powers's office, never even seen them, but I had, and that act had put not only me at risk, but worse, Stella and Avril too, because he had been wearing Stella's orange cap. If I'd had any idea what might happen to those people I loved, I would have given the papers back and signed a pact in blood to never tell a soul about the information those papers contained.

I had not looked at them carefully in Powers's office; there was no time, but I knew they must be important and that there must be something not quite honest about them, something questionable, something that would not be good if it got out about these papers, otherwise Powers would not have seemed so nervous about the possibility that I might see them. If he had not acted so suspicious, I would never have paid the least attention to them—odd, because he was usually very good at dissembling, which is exactly how he had surpassed the other two assistants to George Wanbli, the official, although usually absent, tribal leasing agent.

Even after I took them, I still did not think the papers were of much consequence, probably some small scam Powers and

Wanbli had going, I thought. I was feeling rather self-satisfied that I had gotten my lease check and had not had to wait for it to come in the mail, silly of me, really, because I should have known this would not be the end of it. When the next lease payment was due in January, I would have to fight the same battle all over again, and the tactics that had won this one for me would not work a second time. Still, it felt good to have made a fool of Johnson Powers this one time.

After Stella went to bed on the day I got home from the leasing office, I got out the papers again to have another look, thinking with a little laugh that Johnson and Wanbli and a few others in the tribal offices were probably into something petty—skimming money from the office supplies budget or stealing money from the pop machine and sharing it out, and these ledger sheets were the record of the total take and the disbursements.

Again, I saw that there was a master sheet, a kind of journal with five names on it: George Wanbli and Johnson Powers, of course, and three others. There was Robert Grey, the head of the local branch of the BIA, the Bureau of Indian Affairs, an appointed civil servant, an official of the federal government who, for all practical purposes, had far more authority over tribal policy and decision making than any tribal official. He had veto power, but he had rarely exercised it, usually rubber-stamping whatever decisions the tribal council and tribal council president made. There may have been fights in private, compromising behind closed doors, but at least in public, Grey had given the impression of a benign dictator, a barely visible ghost who sat at the end of the table during tribal council meetings, rarely speaking.

The other two names were Elias Villiers and Mary Denison. Villiers, tribal council president, was no surprise, and Mary Denison should not have been. She was secretary to Johnson Powers, the woman in the outer office who had tried to prevent me from going into Powers's office unannounced, not one of the younger women given jobs they were not competent to handle and not expected to do, but a woman possessed of real administrative skills who had been around the system for several years, knew where the bodies were buried, and knew how to keep them buried. And she was the daughter of Ruby Denison and the niece of Pearl, and that connection told me exactly where those two busybodies had heard the story of the crucified turkey. Now, that connection raised other issues, other questions. Were Ruby and Pearl complicit in whatever scheme was going on here, or only dupes? Probably the latter, I decided, because while both of them were useful for spreading whatever stories the group wanted spread, neither could be trusted not to spill information that the others wanted kept quiet.

Besides the master sheet with the five names on it, there were several ledger sheets for each of the five people with lists of numbers, money, and the totals, but the information in the *item* column did not tell me much. It was enigmatic, a sort of code. There would be a series of three letters with commas in between in the item columns. I knew they weren't acronyms—you know, like BIA where the letters stand for Bureau of Indian Affairs, but these three-letter series had to stand for something. Or maybe, *someone*. They could be people's initials. George Wanbli was the head of the leasing office; Johnson Powers was a deputy in the same office, and Mary Denison was the secretary for the leasing office. It might be reasonable that the initials stood for the names of people whose leases were processed twice a year. I thought through the leasing protocols again.

Originally, years ago, whoever leased land from a Lakota person paid the fees directly to the Indian owner, or to someone, invariably a white person, who was designated as the guardian for the Indian, the assumption being that most Indians were not literate and therefore not competent to handle their own financial dealings. But as more and more Indians became educated, and as complaints came in about guardians who did not pass on the money they collected to the rightful owners, that policy was changed. The tribal leasing office was created to ensure that money was collected and passed on to the Indian owners. It was supposed to be an oversight program, but I wondered, who was overseeing the overseers? In theory, the BIA representative and the tribal council president were supposed to provide oversight, which would be Robert Grey and Elias Villiers. So where did Mary Denison come into it? Easy. She was the person who processed all the payments from the lessees, recorded them, and wrote the checks to the lessors. She handled the money transactions. Just like with the mafia, I thought. If the FBI wants to bring down a mafia family, the person they put the squeeze on is the accountant, because the accountant knows where the money came from and who it went to.

So, it seemed likely that this scheme had to do with skimming money from the lease payments as it passed through the tribal leasing office. Any one of the five people could have thought up the scheme, including Mary, but they all benefited from it. The decision to mail all the lease checks instead of having each landowner collect the payments in person probably had something to do with this scheme. Maybe they were afraid that all of us together in the tribal office at the same time might lead us to discuss with each other the amount of the payment that each of us was getting, to question something about the practices, the procedures, and that might lead to questions they did not want to answer. Safer, then, to just mail the checks, less likely that people would question anything if the amount *seemed* reasonable, seemed close to what each of us was used to getting.

I got the envelope with my lease payment check out of my purse and looked at the amount. It was the same amount as the last check had been, or so I thought. I got my checkbook and looked at the entry for the deposit six months earlier. Same amount. So how could the leasing office be skimming money? I got out the shoe box that held my bank records for the past five years, looked at the biannual deposit amounts for my lease payments. They were all the same. Wait a minute. *They were all the same.* I remembered then something about the payment per acre going up—the amount per acre that each Indian got for leasing their land, so my total payments should have gone up, not stayed the same. And I remembered something else, too, an announcement in the tribal council minutes that the payment per acre would not be going up for all landowners, that the leasing rate would rise only on certain parcels of land, and while some parcels would get increases, some lease payments would actually go down, and therefore, higher lease payments depended on blah, blah, blah. There was some complicated formula, and I did remember also thinking that with my luck, I would not get any increase, so I had not been shocked or surprised when the lease payment was the same as it had been, only relieved that it had not been less.

There is the scam, I thought. There was probably some mandate that the per-acre fee would rise on all Indian-owned land, so we all should have gotten higher payments. These five people were collecting the higher fee from the people who leased the land and not passing it on to the individual tribal owners. They forestalled any possible questions about it by putting out the false story that some lease payments would go down, and then people like me would just be relieved that there had been no cut and not complain about not getting an increase. A very clever scheme. But it might have all fallen apart if people who were in line to pick up their checks had started talking among themselves and discovered that nobody had gotten an increase, but many of the landowners rarely saw each other, so by mailing the checks there was almost no chance that anyone would raise uncomfortable questions. I did a little quick math. I owned 160 acres, and if the increase was $5 per acre, that meant an annual increase of $800, divided by two, each biannual payment would be $400 more. Not a whole lot of money to split up among the five conspirators here, but multiply that amount by all the landowners, some of whom owned far more than 160 acres, and the annual take would run into the hundreds of thousands of dollars. If they skimmed just $800 for each landowner and there were one thousand of us, that would amount to $800,000 in one year!

No wonder the leasing office did not want me throwing a fuss about collecting my check in person! Then other people might complain also, and the scheme could easily fall apart. And then I remembered something else. Elias Villiers's two-year term as tribal council president would expire in November. He had already begun campaigning for reelection, and if that happened, he would be the first tribal council president in our history to be elected to two consecutive terms, but he had a big incentive. If he was not reelected, he could not collect his share of the stolen lease money, even if the new president could be persuaded to go along with the original scheme. He probably would go along—most people are corruptible if the price is high enough—but Elias would not have wanted to give up his share to the new TCP. Indeed, Elias and his people had been handing around a lot of money in the last few months trying to win reelection. Not all the voters were willing to take bribes, but most people can be easily influenced. I remembered Clara Lately saying that Elias had gotten a well put in and water lines run for the people out in Squash Creek District where her sister lived. A few pork projects like that will influence many people's votes, and who would call that bribery? No, they would say, just good politics. That Elias Villiers gets things done for the people, they would say.

But could I prove any of this? And what did those sets of two or three letters mean? I looked again at the sheets, looking for my own initials: HL for Hazel Latour or HAL for Hazel Ann Latour. I did not find them. If the letters stood for initials of landowners, then there should be hundreds of sets of them, but I found only seventeen different combinations, and something else: the three-letter combinations all ended in *D* or *C*. Would they skim money from only seventeen landowners and not the rest? Of course not. Besides, the money amounts listed were too high for only seventeen landowners. One listing was 61,900—dollars, I was sure, although there was no dollar sign, and the item column contained: WCD, SHC, JC. No three individual people would get a total quarterly payment that high, not possible. But what did the letters stand for? Seventeen combinations. And then I had it.

There were seventeen different districts on our reservations, broken up that way for electing tribal officials, for administering schools, providing fire protection (such as it was), and so on. So WCD stood for White Creek District, SHC for Sand Hills Community, and JC for Jackson Community. But why would those three be grouped together? They were not contiguous geographically, but located in different areas of the reservation.

Suppose, though, just suppose that these five coconspirators would have tried to split up the money from their scheme equally. Lease payments were not the same for all land on the reservation because, for instance, if it was good farming land, it would be more valuable to someone wanting to lease it than would the same amount of land that was mostly rocks and trees and suitable only for grazing. It would seem logical that no one of the five would accept the districts that had only the low lease payment land and allow someone else to have all districts with the higher value land. Okay, that made sense.

But there were only these blanket entries, total amounts from two or more districts, which meant there was probably another set of ledger sheets that listed the landowners for each district. There had to be one for SHC, Sand Hills Community, my own district, that would list my lease and everyone else's in the district and how much money was skimmed from each property. And not surprisingly, the ledger sheet with the entries from SHC, my district, were being paid to George Wanbli.

Things fall into place. George was not just an idiot who was jealous because his own reputation and following as a medicine person was on the wane while mine was on the rise. His vindictiveness against me was far deeper. He was worried that I might figure out the scheme, and he was trying to scare me into behaving myself, backing off. Or maybe, convince me that he was a stupid man whose only concern with me was jealousy, a distraction from the real issue.

What could I possibly do about it? I suppose he—and Powers and the others—were worried, or at least concerned. What *could* I possibly do? I could tell everyone I knew. Some people would always side with me, some with Wanbli and his group, and that would mean Elias Villiers would probably not be reelected and the scheme would fall apart. Mary and the rest of them, with the connivance of Robert Grey, could still probably withhold all the information, hide the figures, the facts, such things were done all the time, but it would be a big scandal that would divide the tribe, perhaps even push us into physical violence, one group against another group, and worse yet, groups splintering off until general chaos resulted. I could take it higher than that.

I could report it to the FBI, who had jurisdiction on Indian reservations for any major felonies, but I would need to have evidence. Would these sheets that I had in my possession be enough? I had no idea. I wished I had the other set of ledger sheets, the ones that broke out the individual leaseholders by district.

I did not sleep much that night for thinking about the whole nasty scheme and wondering what I could do about it, what I should do about it. I was angry. I had been cheated and so had every other Indian landowner. If the scheme had only come into being since Elias Villiers had been elected, I had only been cheated out of about $1,600. Only $1,600! For me, that was a great deal of money, money that I could have used to put in that bathroom I wanted and had money to spare. Money I could have used to make life a little bit easier for Stella and me. We could have had more tulips.

And when that money was multiplied by all the other land-owners who had been cheated, the total was shocking. These people are buzzards, I thought, preying on their own people. I wondered, too, about Robert Grey. Was he kicking back some of his share of the money to someone farther up the food chain? Did this scheme exist only on our reservation, or did it go all the way to the head of the BIA in Washington DC?

The more I thought about it, the more frightened I got. This could mean millions of dollars illegally stolen from thousands of people, and people have done ugly things to other people for a lot less than millions. People could be killed.

Finally, finally, I must have fallen asleep. The cow was bawling in the corral, the cats yowling at the back door the next morning because I slept two hours past time to do the milking and feed the cats, and Stella, too, slept on, her face as innocent as a twelve-year-old going on thirteen can be, hand curled under her chin. I did not wake her, but after I had done the milking and fed the cats, I let the chickens and turkeys out of their coop, usually Stella's job. They ran out, chastising me with their clucking when I finally opened their door, except the white turkey, who looked at me as if she knew my secret but had no good advice.

That was silly, I told myself. That turkey was not *wakan*, not a sentient being, human or spiritual. She was only quieter than the other bigmouth chickens and turkeys. But in spite of all my protestations to Stella, I did wish that this was a wise turkey, a spiritual being I could consult as I would a medicine person for advice. I felt like such a fraud. Other people contacted me for advice about their problems, considered me wise, heeded what I told them, but I had no answers for myself. Physician, heal thyself, I thought, but healing is not automatic, does not come because we wish it. I had no clearer ideas of what on earth I should do with the knowledge in my possession and with the documents that were even now wrapped in layers of waxed paper and burrowed deep in the flour bin, a place that I was reasonably sure no one would think to look for them—and by now, Johnson Powers must certainly know they were missing and certainly know who had taken them. By now, he must have told George Wanbli, and all the others, and they must be deciding if the problem they had with me had now grown much more serious and pressing, and if so, what they should do about it.

Was there some message that I was supposed to get from the attack on my animals a few weeks earlier, other than George Wanbli was jealous and angry over my medicine man practice? Or had it just been a generalized terrorism, a way of letting me know that I was vulnerable? There was no way to tell, but with the amount of money involved in this scheme I had discovered, I had no doubt that if there was a future attack, it would go beyond slaughtering my animals.

You had better figure out something smart to do and you had better figure it out fast, I told myself, because these people are not going to let you get away with the theft of papers that could implicate them in a major felony. But what to do?

I turned it over in my mind the rest of the day as I went about my work. I got out my pipe, I lit sage and sweetgrass, and I prayed to the spirits for guidance, and then I let it go, but kept myself quiet and detached, listening. I had to trust there would be an answer and it would come soon.

Stella gave me the occasional sideways glance, but she kept to herself and did not annoy me with questions. She had seen me quiet and withdrawn before when I was praying and meditating on a problem for someone else. We were sitting under the box elder tree snapping green beans when I had an idea, only half an idea, but the only thing that had occurred to me.

"Stella, your birthday is next Sunday. What would you like to do to celebrate?"

She turned her head sideways looking toward the horizon, a green bean half raised toward her face, an expression and gesture so like her mother that it wrung my heart.

"I hadn't thought about it much," she said.

I did not believe her. Going from twelve years old, a child, to thirteen, a teenager moving into adulthood, is such an important passage for everyone that I was sure she had thought about it often and long, but I suspected that her dreams of celebrating the day were fantasies far beyond my capacity to fulfill. Nevertheless, I intended to make it a good day to the best of my ability.

"The chokecherries ought to be ripe about now," I said. Stella savored chokecherry jelly and syrup almost as much as chocolate candy. "I thought if you wanted to, we could go to He Dog Lake for a picnic and check out the chokecherries at the same time."

She snapped the bean, dropped it into the pot on the ground between us, leaning slightly as she did, her long dark brown hair falling across her face, hiding her expression. I thought she would like the idea, sure she would, but an almost teenager does not give away any emotion to their elders that they can help.

"Could we invite Avril to come along too?"

"Sure. Shall we invite all the Latelys? Clara will want to pick chokecherries too, if they are ripe. And Ed loves to fish."

She grimaced. "That means Huey, Dewey, and Louie have to come along too," she said. She was referring to Avril's younger brothers, Melvin, Norris, and Lester.

"Be nice. Do you call them comic book character names to their faces?"

"Sometimes," she admitted. "But they just say mean things back."

I arched an eyebrow at her. "That is rather childish. I think you are you getting a little too old for name calling?"

She did not respond to that.

"I would think you might be interested in being friends with Nancy."

"Nancy's spending the summer with her auntie in Rapid City, so I won't have to put up with her being bossy and stuck up."

I finished snapping the last of the beans, dusted my hands, and picked up the pot. Grandma Lately had gone with Nancy to spend time with her other daughter, Nancy's aunt. I would never directly say so to Stella, but I was glad that Nancy would not be along, and Grandma, too. I respected the old lady, but as deaf and half blind as she was, it was difficult to carry on a conversation with her.

"So, what do you think? Picnic at He Dog with the Latelys?"

She smiled and nodded, as if she had a secret.

I stood up and pulled her to her feet, pot of green beans under one arm, the other arm around her shoulders.

"All right, then. Let's drive over to the Latelys and invite them. Clara would like this mess of beans, too," I said. "We can stop and get the mail on the way."

In the house, I glanced at the old windup Big Ben on the sideboard. Two o'clock. The tribal offices would be open until five.

Sand Hills Community isn't a town, not even a village. There's just the post office with a one-pump gas station next to it, the post office run by the same old lady who had run it for the past ten years since her husband died. Her grandson ran the gas station next door, a perfect job for him since he was lazy and did not have to do much of anything except breathe in gas fumes, fill the pop machine every morning, and take money when customers pumped their own gas a couple of times a day. There is a pay phone on the wall outside the gas station.

I asked Stella to check the mail and gave her change to get

us a couple of bottles of pop, while I went directly to the pay phone, fumbled in my purse for the number of the tribal leasing office. The operator took her own sweet time about telling me how many coins to deposit, but then the phone was ringing and Mary Denison answered.

"Hello, Mary. This is Hazel Latour."

Silence on the other end. I wondered what Mary was thinking, what she had discussed with Johnson and the others.

"Let me put you through to Mr. Powers," she said.

"No, Mary, never mind. I actually want to talk to you."

Again a silence, and then, "What about?" spoken cautiously, suspiciously.

"I accidentally picked up some papers when I was in the office yesterday, and I would like to return them." I put a casual smile in my voice, a silent way of saying what I did not want to put into words—*I've gotten hold of something I want to turn loose of, no hard feelings, you understand.*

"What do you mean?" Mary asked.

She knew very well what I meant, but her tone of voice told me that she—and the others—had no idea how much I had figured out about the papers I had in my possession, and she was not about to enlighten me.

"I want to make an appointment with Mr. Powers, say, for next Monday? I can return the papers then, and discuss another matter with him."

"What matter?"

"Oh," I said. "The usual. Picking up my lease payment in person instead of getting it mailed to me."

"Oh, that," Mary sounded relieved. I thought that she believed me, that she and the others had talked about whether I would figure out the meaning of the information on the ledger sheets, and now, she had decided that I had not, that I had probably picked them up and taken them just for spite, because they were conveniently at hand, because I was a troublemaker, but not a very bright one.

"Mr. Powers has an opening at ten o'clock tomorrow," she said.

I hesitated, as if I was thinking about it, and then I said, "Oh, Mary, I have a bunch of stuff coming ready in my garden this week. You know how it is when everything comes ready at once—picking, washing, canning. I will be really busy. I was really planning on next Monday. Would ten o'clock on Monday work?"

More silence. I knew she was thinking; I hoped she was thinking that if I was in no hurry to get it back, so casual, that I had no idea of what I had gotten hold of.

"Yes. That would be fine," she said. "Ten o'clock on Monday, the eleventh."

"Good, then," I said brightly. "Say hello to your Aunt Ruby and Aunt Pearl for me." And then, I did something wicked, perverse, and childish, something that had nothing whatsoever to do with returning the papers, ending the leasing scam, or anything other than my own desire to stir trouble. I said, "By the way, you might tell Ruby and Pearl that what they heard about the white turkey is all true. It was crucified. It was dead. I saw it, and I buried it with my own hands, and three hours later it rose from the dead. Tell them that it is all true. Do you have that, Mary? Tell them it is all true. Okay. See you next Monday."

In truth, waiting almost a week to turn in the papers was not intended to make Mary think I did not know what they meant, although if she got that notion, good. The truth was I had no idea what I would say to Johnson Powers. I needed the time to figure it all out, and that nonsense about the resurrection of the white turkey was only a distraction.

On Sunday I went with Stella and the Latelys to He Dog Lake feeling that I had finally figured out exactly what I would do, how I could put an end to the leasing scam without any serious repercussions. I was going to tell Johnson Powers that I knew exactly what the ledger sheets meant, exactly who was involved. I was going to blackmail him, tell him that if the thieving stopped immediately, if future leasing payments reflected the legal raises in the per-acre payments and were handed out to landowners who collected the money in person, I would keep my mouth shut about the money they had already stolen. And to insure that they stopped stealing, I was going to tell him, I had made copies of the ledger sheets that I was handing back. In retrospect, it was a stupid plan, something out of a plot in a movie or a bad detective novel. Millions had been stolen, and there were potentially millions more to be had, so why should these people let one middle-aged woman ruin all that? People *have* been killed for far less, and that is not just some plot from a movie.

However, I had no chance to put the plan into play because on Sunday afternoon, Avril Lately was kidnapped from He Dog Lake.

12 Hazel

Clara Lately was a good woman, but a strong personality, or to be blunt, a nagging wife, taught well by her mother, and together teaching Nancy Lately to be the same, not directly teaching, mind you, not with a regular lesson plan, but by example. Ed Lately's passive personality did not mean that he was henpecked but did mean that he saw keeping his mouth shut and pretending to be dumber than he was as the path of least resistance. Given the opportunity, Ed could be a very effective and competent human being, especially when Clara was not around, which was part of the reason I insisted that she take the children and go report Avril's absence to the tribal police.

As soon as the Latelys' car carried Clara and the children over the hill and out of sight, I turned to Ed.

"Where do you think we should start looking?" I asked. I find that asking a direct, simple question can often make people focus on a problem.

He slowly eased himself down on the spot with the deepest grass, took off his cap, and rubbed his rough hand through his hair, a thinking gesture.

I sat down, too.

"You and Clara saw him last," he said. "What direction was he heading? Did he say anything?"

"We were down there," I said, pointing south along the lake bank, "where those two big chokecherry trees are. He came from this direction. He stopped and picked a few handfuls of berries, but Clara and I were talking so we did not pay him much attention. When I looked around, he was walking south again into the thicker woods along the lake bank."

Ed nodded.

"There're places along there where the brush comes right down to the edge of the lake and the bank drops off steep below that. He could've fallen in."

He did not complete the thought—and *drowned*—but we were both thinking of it.

"We need to search along that bank first," he said.

I stood up and said, "Time to begin. We only have a few more hours before dark."

Neither of us said anything as we walked south past the now stripped chokecherry trees, the grass trampled beneath from where Clara and I had stood, one branch still bent from where we pulled it down to get the fruit at the top. As we approached the place where the woods got thicker, the sound of a small outboard motor came from the lake, and there, fifty yards out in the water, was a small fishing boat with two men in it, fishing poles extended, the boat moving slowly. One of the men was older, one younger, but there was a distinct resemblance in the set of their rounded shoulders, the set of their necks, even the angle of their cap bills. Probably a father and son.

"Hey," Ed hollered at them.

They waved back and throttled the motor back to nothing. A light breeze sent ripples of water slapping against the shiny aluminum side of the boat.

"We're looking for a lost kid," Ed hollered. "Boy in jeans and a white tee shirt and an orange cap, about this high." He measured with his hand, too short, but then, I have never known a man yet who knew the exact size of his own children; always they over or underestimate.

The two men exchanged glances, shook their heads.

"How long has he been missing?" the older man asked.

"Two, three hours," Ed responded. "We've got no trace of him. Gonna get dark in a while."

"Yeah," the older man said. "We can take a cruise up and down this bank here and look if that would be of any use to you."

"Sure would," Ed said. "I'd appreciate any help. We sent my wife to notify the tribal police, but it'll be a while before they get here."

"Why don't you get in the boat with us? You might spot the boy before either of us would," the older man said.

Ed looked at me, and I nodded.

"You go on with them," I said. "I will stay here and look around some more, and be here when the police come."

"All right, then."

The men rowed the boat into the shore, and Ed gave a leap of faith and landed in the middle.

The older man put out his hand.

"I'm Tom Wallace from Mission. That's my son, Wayne."

Ed shook hands with them both, then the boat moved off slowly fifteen feet out from the bank. I walked on to where the woods got thicker in a ragged edge between a sort of meadow with random cottonwood, elm, and lighter brush that ran up to and over the edge of the ridge several hundred yards to the west. I did not go into the brush, no point because I could tell if someone had gone in. The brush would have been smashed down somewhat and pushed aside, but I saw nothing to indicate anyone had entered the woods at any point. Avril must have turned and gone up the ridge, but there was no trail, no sign that he had been there. There is this misconception that an Indian, any Indian, all Indians, can track a bug over solid rock, or at least anything bigger than a rabbit over normal ground with grass and a few trees and so on, but I never knew any Indians who were trackers, and I sure was not one. I have such a poor sense of direction that I get turned around all the time. When I was a young girl, my mother used to say that it was a good thing I was not born a hundred years ago because if I had been and had gone off alone from the camp, my sense of direction was so poor I would have wandered around on the prairies until I starved to death.

I walked to the top of the ridge, through occasional patches of brush, around a few big trees, avoiding a few patches of poison ivy, thinking that I would be happy to have Avril back even if he came back covered in poison ivy. That was a problem I knew how to fix. I did not think of Johnson Powers, of George Wanbli and Mary Denison and the others; that they might have had anything to do with Avril's disappearance did not even enter my head, a foolish naïveté that I would regret, along with the impulse that caused me to steal those ledger sheets. All my life I have had to pay for my own arrogance. It was unfair that others had to pay the price for my own shortcomings.

At the top of the hill, I sat down and looked at the land spread out in a fan of green dotted with trees to my left, the heavier brush and trees to the right, searching for anything that might look like a sleeping boy, an unconscious boy, but I saw nothing. Out on the lake, I sometimes caught glimpses in between the intervening trees of the boat, the sun reflecting off it, with the men in it in as it trolled slowly along the lake shore going south, and then farther down, going east across the narrow neck in the lake to the east bank. I was comforted. If the boat had not stopped, the men had not found a body floating in the lake. Behind me to the west, the sun had dropped another notch in the sky. It would be dark in less than two hours.

Stella's thirteenth birthday, an invitation to adulthood, to womanhood, a day I had meant to be an easing into that new world, that new phase in her life would now be, no matter how this turned out, an event that she would recall in later years as a nightmare crossing.

I remembered my own childhood, the many times that I had played on the shores of this very lake while the men of the family fished and the women gathered chokecherries and sometimes wild plums. I remembered roaming these hills, being kissed for the first time by John Latour when he was fourteen and I was eleven, too young for a boyfriend and too precocious to care. It was right down there, I thought, down there a hundred yards or so beyond the chokecherry trees that Clara and I had stripped earlier, and another hundred yards up the ridge by a cut bank where the water had carved out that little cave from the limestone.

The limestone cave! How many generations of children thought they had discovered something that no one else had, and how many wise parents had let them think so, knowing that those discoveries are made over and over and every discovery, no matter how old, is new and important to those who made it.

I got up, dusted off my pants, and started down the hill, knowing where Avril would be. It was not that easy to find the cave coming down from the ridge instead of up from the lake, so I walked past it, turned, looked at the sky and the arrangements of the trees, older than me by many, many years, caught my bearings—who said I had no sense of direction—and saw the trampled path through the knee-high brush, the weeds hanging down and the dark entrance, and there, beneath a bush, not Avril but the orange cap that Stella had been wearing and had given to him.

I snatched it up and looked at it carefully, but there was no blood on it, only some dirt and the smudging that could have been fingerprints, Stella's or Avril's, who would know? I bent down and looked inside the shallow cave, but there was nothing inside, nothing at all. I walked, no ran, around through the weeds, the grass, the brush, pushing it aside, tearing my hands on the brambles, knowing that only a jackrabbit or a gopher was small enough to hide itself here. Could Avril have thrown off the cap and went in chase of a rabbit? Of course not, stupid, I told myself. He is a kid, not a goddamned dog. But where could he be? And, of course, of course, the answer had to be that Avril had not gone off by himself, that he had come only as far as this cave, that someone had found him and taken him away, someone who saw the orange hat and thought they were stealing my granddaughter and got Avril by mistake. Someone too stupid to know or pay close enough attention to know that a twelve-year-old with long hair and dressed in jeans could be either a boy or a girl. Someone who had silenced Avril soon enough so they would not know from his voice and his words that they had gotten the wrong kid, probably shoved him into a big gunny sack and never taken a second look.

This was my fault. I had invited this with my own arrogance, my own stupidity, my own foolish confidence that I could stop a group of people willing to risk a great deal to steal millions of dollars from their own people. I might even have gotten Avril killed, and how, *how*, could I ever explain it to Ed and Clara, to Stella, to myself? I was sick, sick of myself, sick of what we Indians do to each other, sick of being an Indian. In that moment I wanted to walk down to the lake, to step into the dark, rippling waters, to feel the thick tarry mud of the bottom, to bury myself and this orange cap in that sucking mud, to forget all my pretensions of being a medicine person, a person capable of intervening with the spirits on behalf of others, when all I was doing was meddling with forces I had no ability whatsoever to control. I had no faith in anything anymore.

I cried.

When I had done, I walked back to the top of the ridge and

waited. Half an hour later, a tribal police car came slowly up the road. The doors opened, dumped out four crapulous Indian men in filthy clothes and one very tall skinny policeman in a spic-and-span uniform.

"Alfred Black Horse, ma'am," the cop said, sticking out his hand. "I hear you've got a missing kid somewhere out here."

I did not know where to start, did not know how much I should say. I said only, "Avril Lately. His mother is the woman who came in to report it. His father is out on the lake with some fisherman in a boat looking for him. But I've just come across this cap"—I held it out—"so I'm pretty sure he is not in the lake." Or so I hoped. Would whoever have taken him simply pitched him in, sack and all, like disposing of a batch of unwanted kittens?

Albert took the cap, glanced at it, and handed it back. The other men stood around looking like death warmed over. One of them leaned against the car, his eyes closed. I figured they had emptied the jail to get these guys to help search. They would not be much use in the condition they were in, especially if they came up against the people who had taken Avril.

"Any other sign of the kid?"

"I think he has been kidnapped," I said.

A little smile curved up the corners of Alfred's thin-lipped mouth. He glanced at me, glanced quickly away, trying not to laugh, I could tell.

"Mrs.—??"

"Latour. I'm Hazel Latour. A friend of the family."

"Mrs. Latour. All the time, at least three times every summer, a kid goes missing up here. They wander off. They fall down and get hurt. They run off. They always turn up again when they get hungry. They don't get themselves kidnapped."

"I think this one has been kidnapped," I said. I did not say how; I was afraid to say why; I could not give him any details to convince him.

The two-way radio in his car came to life. Alfred raised a finger at me, a signal to wait, went back to the car, and thumbed the button on the handset. One of the men, a young man who would be handsome when he had enough sleep to get the red out of his eyes and enough soap to wash the stink off himself and his clothes, nodded at me.

"*Ina. Ho eyes tokeske oyaunyanpi he.*"

"*Otehe.* I've been better," I said. "Me and mine have been a lot better."

His eyes looked through me. I knew that he was only being polite, that the content of what I said held no meaning for him. He only wanted a bed and relief.

Alfred talked on the two-way, hung up the handset.

"Mrs. Latour. You know of a place called Nellie's Nightie?"

"Nellie's Nightie!" A picture of that run-down house before the turnoff to the lake came into my head. "Yes, I think it used to be the old Bear Claw place."

"Bear Claw? I don't think I know that name. Maybe you mean Bear Paw? That old pink run-down house along the highway. Someone back at the station says we should look at Nellie's Nightie," he said.

"I am ready," I said.

The men all piled back in the car, all four of them in the back behind the security screen, me in front crowded by all the piles of paperwork, empty paper sacks, and old soda bottles. There were enough to get back a deposit of a couple of dollars or more, a treasure trove for Stella. Or Avril.

From the backseat, the smell of unwashed bodies and alcohol oozing out of their pores took me back to my younger days when I was wild and foolish and had gotten myself thrown in the drunk tank that New Year's Eve in Jackson. Much to my shame, my father had bailed me out. No month of working off my fine on garbage pickup.

Alfred turned the car around, getting the rear wheels off the track into the sandy dirt; the rear wheels spun, the transmission groaned and whined, but then he gunned the motor; the car lurched and we went flying down the road, the men in the back packed in too tight to bounce around. I opened each of the three gates because the men could not get out—no handles on the inside of the car doors—frustrated at the necessity, not bothering to follow custom and close them again. If a cop cannot absolve you of the rule, nobody can.

Dust boiled up around the car as Alfred slid it to a stop in the front yard. Up close, the pink house known as Nellie's Nightie was not solid pink, but lighter in places, as if there had not been enough paint for an even single coat, and streaked with rusty lines from water running off the metal roof. The unpainted front door stood slightly ajar as Albert, hand on the pistol in his belt, pushed it open. The men were stuck in the car. I followed Alfred, seeing over his shoulder the interior dimly lit with shafts of light through cracks in the boarded-over windows. There was nothing in the first room except beer cans and liquor bottles, old faded newspapers that had been used as wallpaper, torn now and hanging down in strips. The place smelled of mold and mouse piss. A door led off to another room, darker because it was on the east side of the house, where the late afternoon sun did not come directly through the cracks.

Alfred kept motioning me to stay behind him, putting his fingers to his lips for me to be quiet as if no one would hear the sound of the old rough floor creaking beneath our feet. The next room, too, was empty, except for the same detritus of old parties. Probably a former kitchen, there was a sort of countertop built in along one wall, now broken through in places. Attached to the north side of the house, there was a tiny lean-to room probably a pantry because it had no windows. I pushed past Alfred. There behind a battered white door hanging partly off the hinges was a heap of old burlap sacks with Avril nested in the middle, bent into a circle like the pictures of the snake eating its own tail.

I must have made some sound because Alfred crowded in behind me. Avril was warm.

I held him in my arms, rocking him like a baby all the way into the hospital in Mission. I made promises that I had every intention of keeping to every god and spirit I knew of, even though I do not believe in Jesus or Mohammed. I picked twigs and shreds of burlap from his hair. I stroked his face, around the big purple knot at his left temple, the swollen left eye. I whispered in his ear. I anointed his face with tears that spotted the dirt.

When I got out of the car after the emergency people at the hospital had taken him from me, I fell on my knees, my legs temporarily paralyzed from his weight. Albert helped me up, started to walk inside, but turned back when the men in the backseat of the car pounded on the window to be let out.

Emergency waiting rooms are all the same no matter the décor, no matter where they are. There are the same outdated magazines, dog-eared with coupons torn out; the same tired and hungry crying babies and bratty little kids running around and over people's feet, screaming and fighting; the same serious gray-faced adults waiting to be seen by a doctor, a nurse, please god, anyone, even a goddamned janitor will do because, oh Christ, it hurts and at this point they would rather die than sit there; and people like me waiting for word from someone authority inside about someone they love, or maybe someone they hurt, or someone they wronged, and feeling guilt and despair and believing that the waiting will go on and on for all eternity and someday in some far-distant future, an archeologist from another planet will unearth this waiting room, and one of the gray-faced people will look up and say, "Is it my turn?"

Sometime later, much later, Alfred brought Ed Lately in. I had forgotten completely about him circling the lake in that little boat with the two fisherman. After I told him that Avril was inside, that no one had told me anything, he nodded. He had been in emergency waiting rooms before.

"When they let me out on the bank by the picnic area, I couldn't find you," he said, clasping my hands in a show of emotion that I never expected. "I thought you were gone, too. I would have taken your car to go look for you, but I didn't have the keys."

In a little while, Clara and all the kids came in, Clara fluttering and questioning over and over, repeating herself until Ed, maybe for the first time in his life, said, "Clara, shut up," but gently, as he put his arm around her and pulled her as close as the chair arms between them would allow, her face and mouth muffled against his old blue chambray shirt.

The Lately kids joined the other little kids running and screaming and tripping each other. Stella sat beside me, silent as a stone. I pulled the orange cap from my purse, where I had stowed it, and handed it to her.

When the nurse banged open the swinging door to the back and stuck her head into the waiting room, everyone looked up, expectant as starving dogs waiting to be fed.

"Lately?" she said, and I was stuck with the stupid, stupid impulse to say, "Well, not lately!" but we all rose as if walking down a church aisle for communion, full of awe and dread and glad of the company of others, the starving dog–like impulses quelled, but our guts growling for the nourishment of information and not of communion.

"Come with me," she said, and we all followed her down a long, long waxed floor corridor to a little room where she stood aside, and we crowded in. A harried looking young man sat behind a desk, his hair rumpled as if he had just yanked off one of those caps that doctors wear in surgery, but at least there was no blood on his green scrubs.

He looked up from scribbling on some report, put his pen down.

"The boy has a concussion, probably the result of the contusion on his left temple, but he has no other signs of trauma, no broken bones or cuts, only a few scrapes and bruises. He regained consciousness but has no memory of what happened to him."

Clara and Ed exchanged a glance of relief. The doctor picked up the pen and rotated it end for end in his hands.

"He is somewhat disoriented and rambling. He kept talking about white turkeys. I think he'll be fine, but I want to keep him overnight for observation. I need you to sign some papers and take them down to the business office, and then you can see him, if you keep it brief."

"Can't we stay with him?" Clara asked.

"Parents only," he said. "No children."

I touched Clara on the shoulder. "If the cops can take me back to the lake so I can get my car, I'll take the boys home with me," I said.

She nodded absently.

The sun rose in the rearview mirror as I drove west from the lake, the boys already sleeping in the back of the car, Stella wide awake in the front seat beside me.

"Hell of a birthday, little one," I said to her.

"I'm no longer a little one," she said calmly.

"No. You are not. Stella—"

"I know," she interrupted. "None of this is my fault. But if I hadn't given him this orange cap, it would be me instead of him. Don't baby me."

"You're right," I said. "But this will get sorted out."

It is not your fault, Stella, I thought, but it is mine, and I have to fix it.

I stopped at the gas station on the way home and used the pay phone to call Mary Denison. I told her that I could not be at the meeting, she would understand why, and then I made other arrangements with her. I asked her to tell George Wanbli that there would be a ceremony at my house on the next Saturday night that I needed him to attend. I knew he would not be able to resist and that Johnson Powers and the others would not do any more foolish things before then.

13 Hazel

Avril was released from the hospital on Tuesday morning, and immediately after Ed and Clara brought him home, Ed came over to collect the three boys who seemed uninterested in Avril once they found out he was okay, but were more interested in which one of them would get to ride in the front seat. Ed solved it by putting Melvin in front. He stood outside the car trying to talk to me while the two in the back seat shouted insults at Melvin reaching over the seat to pummel him.

"He does seem to be fine now," Ed said in between yelling at the boys.

"*Waste,*" I said. "But does he remember anything more about what happened to him?"

"No. He says he was inside that little cave and decided to go back to get Stella. He started to crawl out, and that's the last he remembers." He hesitated a minute before going on. "I wish he could remember what happened. It seems awful odd that he would fall down and hurt himself just enough to be addled and then wander off down to that house and go to sleep there. It's at least three miles down there through several gates, and him with a big old knot on his head."

I could not tell him the truth, at least not yet.

"Kids do odd things," I said, knowing it was a platitude. "He is going to be fine, and that is the good thing."

"Yeah. But it was sure—" Here he stopped, leaned into the window, and cuffed at the two boys in the back seat. "I SAID knock it off!"

I glanced over the top of the car and met Stella's eyes, where she was standing on the other side trying to talk to Melvin in the front seat. She rolled her eyes and walked off toward the garden. I looked at her stiff back and thought that with all the problems of raising her, I was glad my daughter had birthed one girl, not one girl and four boys. I thought how much I loved this child, *takoja*, no longer a child, not yet a woman, but a person moving between two stages of life leaving one behind and growing into a new body and a new knowledge of who she was. In that moment I decided that I would have to tell her about everything, the leasing scam, the people involved. If not for her gift of her orange cap to Avril, I might not be talking to Ed about Avril's health, but to a doctor about Stella, or worse. She deserved to know the truth and to have some part in determining the outcome.

"I'd better get these kids home before they kill each other," Ed said as he opened the door and got in the car.

"Tell Clara we will be over this afternoon to see Avril," I said.

He nodded, started the car, and drove off.

Stella wanted to bring something to Avril, so she made him a cake, chocolate with chocolate icing, except she saved a little out that did not have cocoa in it, wrote on top in butter-colored words "Get Well." It seemed to me that he was already well, but Clara would not let him get up and run around. I probably would have done the same if it had been Stella. We sat in Clara's living room, Avril lying on the old leather sofa with the stuffing coming out in spots where the quilts did not cover. Stella sat on the floor, the three little boys giggling and shoving chocolate cake in each other's faces until Clara made them go outside.

"It is good to see you okay, Avril," I said when Clara took our plates to the kitchen. "The doctor said you were talking about seeing the white turkey."

He plucked at a string on the quilt.

"Yeah. I don't remember much. Just, I was coming out of the cave—" He looked at Stella as if to reassure himself that the adults already knew about the cave, so he was not revealing a secret, "I was coming out of the cave to go get Stella. I don't remember what happened. But I thought I saw the white turkey right in front of me. She was gobbling, kind of, and her wings were all spread and there was this light behind her so she glowed kind of. I felt like she was, you know, protecting me." He said these last two words very low, embarrassed.

"Protecting you from what?" I asked.

He shrugged his shoulders.

"I dunno. Whatever. Bad things."

"Did you feel like something bad was happening to you?"

He was silent a minute, now winding the loose string from the quilt around and around his finger.

"Not really. I dunno. Maybe."

"Did you feel scared?"

"No. Not until I woke up in the hospital." He looked up at me, more animated and sure of his words. "When I woke up, I thought the white turkey was hovering over me, and then the light kind of cleared up, and I saw it was a woman in white, a nurse, I guess."

Well, that was strange, I thought. Of course, it was ridiculous; the white turkey had been home pecking dirt in my front yard. The entire Lately family including Avril had that nonsensical notion that the white turkey was a sacred being, *wakan*, so I suppose that while some Christians might see images of Jesus in a time of great stress, it was probably just as natural for Avril to see the white turkey. Under ordinary circumstances, I would have wished that Avril did not talk about that experience, did not repeat something that was obviously the product of a disordered mind trying to create sense and order out of a confusing and painful circumstance. But this time, this one time, I thought Avril's vision might have use. Going home, Stella and I drove five miles out of our way to visit Pearl and Ruby Denison.

There is an old saying that a lie will travel around the world before the truth can get out of sight. Gossip, belonging to that special category of neither truth nor lie, but partaking of both, can travel twice as fast, at least. On Thursday afternoon when I went to pick up my mail at the post office, Mrs. Henry, the postmaster, asked me if it was true that the Great White Turkey had abducted Avril Lately from the shores of He Dog Lake, transported him miles away, and revealed wonders to him in a vision.

I said I did not know, but if so, my white turkey had no part in it. She paid no attention to what I said—probably did not really want to hear anything I had to say, only to pass on to me what she had heard, what she had misheard, and what she had embroidered like a crazy quilt.

That Lately boy, she said, had a visitation from a sacred being, a white turkey, and the turkey had told him that there were evil ones living among the Lakota, evil spirits disguised as people we had known all our lives, and those evil people were stealing.

"Stealing what?" I asked.

She was not clear on that.

"Well, stealing land, of course! Isn't that what every *wasicu* always wants?" she said, her skinny, bent body going rigid and upright, her chin poked out and her eyes ablaze.

"*Wasicu*? White people? I thought it was evil spirits in Indian people who were stealing."

"Aren't they the same thing?" she demanded.

"Got me there, Mrs. Henry," I admitted. "Did the sacred white turkey tell the Lately boy what people have been taken over by evil spirits?"

She moved closer to me, looked from side to side, beckoned me.

I leaned over and put my ear close to her mouth.

"George Wanbli and Elias Villiers," she whispered.

I jerked back.

"No!"

She nodded satisfaction.

"Yes."

"Did the—umm—*sacred* white turkey tell him what to do about it?" I asked.

She clicked her mouth and turned away.

"Well, that's not the way spirits work, now is it? They send you a vision and it's not just a vision for you, but for the people, so you have to tell it, and that's what that Lately boy did."

So far, the story was not exactly what I had started when I told it to Ruby and Pearl but close enough. Then Mrs. Henry told me about the cloud that the turkey had taken Avril to, how the turkey had put her wing around his shoulder and told him that he was to be a watcher, a protector of his people, and that he would come into possession of great powers someday, and that he had to use those powers to protect all the people. That part was embroidery. I never said anything of the kind, but I know that gossip is like gossip—any story, no matter how simple, gets bigger and fancier with every telling. I had counted on it.

Stella helped me go through all the herbs I had, sorting what we would need, what had been dried too long and needed replacing, helped me look in the fields and along the road ditches for fresher ones. We went over everything in our plan again and again, taking the different parts of the people—me, her, George. We considered whether Johnson Powers would show up and if he would walk right in with George or if he would hang back for some reason they might plot together. We thought out every detail, over and over, and Stella went along with everything until early on Saturday morning, when I took the hatchet and started for the coop to let all of the chickens and all the turkeys out, except for one of the young turkey hens, a brown and black one; she had insisted that it could not be a white one.

I started to open the coop door, but she held my arm, the one that grasped the hatchet.

"Hazel," she said, and no more than that, but I could see the anguish in her eyes, the questions that she had.

"Stella. We agreed. You agreed. I know you have some belief that the mother turkey, the white mother turkey is—is special. I think someday you will know that is not true, but for now, it is okay to think that. And I agreed that I would not touch even the young white turkey hens, only the brown and black one."

She pulled her lips in, making a thin line of her mouth.

"It is only a bird. Food. You have helped me kill dozens and dozens of chickens. This is just like that. You do not have to help."

She let go my arm, and walked off, her shoulders heaving silently. I did not go to her. Together we mixed up flour and water and lard, rolled it out to make a piecrust. Stella chopped up rhubarb. We boiled it up in a pan with sugar and the few strawberries from the garden that the birds hadn't found, put the pie in the oven and while it was baking, we got out the big pan of cornbread that I had baked the previous night, crumbled it with chopped onions from the garden, and some celery seed because we don't grow that and there was none fresh available in town at the grocery store. We mixed it up with some broth from a boiled chicken, some butter, and then we added the salt and paper, the sage, put it inside the bird, and slid it into the oven. The turkey was small, not full grown yet, but big enough to do for my purposes.

We boiled up some chokecherries with plenty of sugar until

they jelled, set them aside to cool. I scrubbed sweet potatoes and sliced them, put them in a flat glass dish, and Stella sprinkled them with brown sugar and dotted them with butter. And then, we carefully mixed up a pitcher of red Kool-Aid with half the water and no sugar, added a little red wine, the contents of two iron supplement capsules, and a big dose of a special herb, one that I rarely used, and then only sparingly. Then the two of us sat under the box elder tree for a few minutes, drinking iced tea as we waited.

Just at sundown, when the house had begun to smell like thanksgiving, we rushed through the chores. Stella helped me catch the white turkey, who put up no resistance, looking at us with those beady, blinking eyes. We tied her feet together, pulled a gunny sack up over her from her feet and bunched it around her neck so she couldn't flap her wings, wrapped a heavy duty rubber band around her beak to silence her, and put her in the pantry. Then we moved the kitchen table around so that one end of the table was right in front of the closed pantry door, allowing just enough room for the door to open.

Just before the time I had told Mary that the ceremony would start, we put out plates and silverware and glasses for two people, laid out all the food on the table, with the roasted turkey in the middle in the place of honor and the jug of iced Kool-Aid sitting by my place.

When we heard a car motor coming up the driveway, Stella got into the pantry with the turkey, pulling the door not quite shut behind her.

George got out of his car, a new black Cadillac that he would have had to go to Rapid City to buy since there were no dealerships on the rez or even in Jackson. He stood there, looking around nervously, so I tried to put him at ease.

I opened the screen door and stepped out onto the porch.

"Thank you for coming, George," I said. "I really appreciate it."

He still hung back by his car, as if ready to make an instant escape. I saw no one inside, but I walked out to stand beside him so I could sneak a peek into the backseat. There was no one hiding there, no Benny or anyone else.

"What kind of ceremony is this?" George asked.

"A ceremony to ask for protection. And the granting of favors," I said.

I knew he wanted explanation but was reluctant to ask. I knew that he was nervous after the attempt to kidnap Stella had gone so far awry, that he was nervous, yes, knowing that I knew what he had intended to do, that he—or the people he had sent to do it—had messed up, wondering if I had told anybody in authority, worried of consequences but curious, too, and looking for a way out, no longer sure of his own ability to control whatever knowledge I might have. I tried to put him at ease, to give him a sense of security.

"I have asked you here in a spirit of cooperation," I lied. "We have had differences in the past, but I am sure we can work them out to the satisfaction of all concerned."

He put on a hesitant little smile.

"I hope that we can come to some—agreement," he said.

I waved my hand as if batting away a minor issue, a fly, something of no consequence.

"Oh, of course! Certainly we can. Please, come in. I have everything prepared. I think you will like this ceremony, and the feast I have prepared."

He started toward the front door. I hurried around him, up the porch step, and opened the door with a comic, sweeping gesture. He stepped inside, glancing around, his eyes coming to rest on the table loaded with food. The room was dim, only the lamp turned low in the middle of the table providing a flickering light.

I pulled out the chair at the end of the table, the one with the back to the pantry door where Stella hid with the white turkey.

"Here," I said. "Please sit."

He took the seat, slid the chair closer to the table, and breathed deep.

"It smells wonderful," he said.

"Glad you think so," I said. I poured a glass of the red Kool-Aid mixture, handed it to him, poured myself another, holding my hand to disguise how little my glass contained. "To our association, to our peaceful cooperation."

I raised the glass to my lips but did not take a drink. George drank a third of the glass, held it away from him, and looked at it.

"What is this?" he asked.

"A spirit drink," I said. "Nothing harmful at all. Only Kool-Aid with a little wine."

He took another sip.

"Not bad. Nice and cool." His eyes were already greedily devouring the food.

"We will eat in a bit, but first we have some business to discuss, then if we are in agreement, and I think we will both be satisfied, then the ceremony."

I reached into my pocket and took out the folded ledger pages that I had taken from Johnson Powers's office and held them out to George.

"Do you know what these are?" I asked.

He glanced at them but refused to take the papers, unsure of what to admit.

I tapped them against my hand.

"Let me tell you," I said. "These are records of money that has been skimmed from lease payments to tribal landowners."

His face was blank, a façade, I knew. I doubt if he paid much attention to the record-keeping side of things, probably would not have known exactly what the original ledger sheets looked like, and in this dim light would be much more uncertain, but he would have seen similar records, would have insisted upon it to make sure he was getting his cut.

"I had no idea what these were when I took them. But I figured it out. My math says that this is worth close to a million dollars or more a year, to the five of you, the ones whose names are on these papers. My heart says you should all be sent to prison for a long time for this."

He started to speak but I swept my hand forward and slapped his mouth with the papers.

"You need to listen to me!" I said loudly. He sat back in his chair abruptly. It seemed to me that his head wobbled a bit on his shoulders.

I stepped away a few feet. It is unwise to push someone beyond their boundaries; even a cornered jackrabbit will fight. George was much bigger and more powerful than a rabbit, not yet completely disarmed.

"My heart says you should be in prison. My head says that if I took these papers to the FBI, you and Johnson and the others would dither, destroy evidence, stall, and the FBI, being the inefficient boobs that they are, would stumble around and take forever. You would eventually be prosecuted. All of you. My head says this is so, but it also says that you and Mary Denison and Elias Villiers have a lot of relatives and friends that could be persuaded to do very unpleasant things to me and my family and friends. The sort of things that you have already tried."

He pretended to be indignant.

"I had nothing to do with that!"

"Ridiculous. It does not matter which one of you ordered it, you are all complicit. My point is that I know I cannot always protect my family and friends. So I have a compromise to offer."

He glanced around the room as if looking for an escape and, seeing none, took a long drink of his Kool-Aid.

"I can't speak for everyone, but let me hear it," he said.

"I keep my mouth shut. Forget about the money you have already stolen, but your scheme stops as of now. No more skimming;

every landowner gets their payments raised as of next issue date to reflect the raise the BIA authorized a year ago. I give you these papers I have here."

I saw the machinations going on behind his eyes. I saw him trying to organize his thinking. He was thinking that if I gave him the papers, I would have no proof at all. The scheme could continue. If I went to the FBI without evidence, they would listen politely to any complaint I might make, but would do nothing, investigate nothing.

"In return for these papers, you go through a ceremony with me where you swear to the spirits that you will abide by our agreement."

That took him aback. George was a vile man, a thief, a bully, but I was convinced that he did believe in the spirit world, did believe that violations of promises made in ceremony would cause him great harm. I was counting on that, but also counting on the special ceremony that I would perform to make sure he kept his promise.

"Do you agree?"

I could tell he was reluctant, that he had other thoughts in his head.

"If you are thinking I would be stupid enough to invite you here without any protection, without any alternative plan in case you got—pushy, you are very mistaken," I said.

"I don't know what you're talking about," he said. He tipped up his glass and drank it all.

I laughed.

"Of course, you know what I am talking about," I said. "This is the original set of papers. I have a copy that someone else has in a safe place. If I turn up dead, those papers and an explanatory letter will automatically be mailed to the FBI office in Rapid City. If you agree to my terms, we go through the ceremony, and I mail the copy of these papers to your office."

"How do I know that you haven't made a third copy?"

I shrugged. "How do I know you will abide by any agreements you make with me today? I do not know. Neither do you know if you can trust me, and that is why we'll perform this ceremony. If either of us reneges, it will be up to the spirits to set the punishment for the transgressor and carry it out."

I could see he still felt that there might be a way around making a deal. I knew there was not.

He put out his hand, and I shook it. I poured him another glass and topped up my own half-full one, raised it to him, and said, "To our agreement."

He tipped his up and drank half of it. I took only a tiny sip.

From the sideboard I took a plate of mixed sweetgrass, sage, and cedar and lit it with a match. The fragrant smoke drifted upward in the dim light of the lamp. I sat at the opposite end of the table and began the prayer to *Tunkasila*, a prayer with many variations, one that I knew he had heard, had said, himself hundreds of times, but halfway through the prayer I began to deviate from the usual form.

"—and we thank you, *Tunkasila*, too, for the gift of the white turkey, the sacred white turkey that you sent to guide us . . ."

I went on in this vein for a few minutes. I talked about the miraculous first appearance of the white turkey, the omniscience of the white turkey, the holiness of the white turkey—after all, she had been crucified and risen from the dead. I thanked *Tunkasila* several times for sending the white turkey to reveal hypocrisy among our own people. I knew George was about to lose his composure—I was talking about things that he could not be expected to believe. He deeply believed in the spirit world, but this business of the white turkey would have been too much even for George to accept. I judged the length of the prayer and the depth of the bullshit to just before I knew he would stand up, snatch the papers, and leave.

"*Pilamaya ye, Tunkasila*, for all these things and more. Observe what I do," I said.

Then I stood up, lifted the plate of burning sweetgrass, sage, and cedar in one hand, the papers in the other, and ceremoniously touched the corner of the papers to the embers in the dish. The corner crinkled, blackened, and flames crept upward.

I sat the plate on the table in front of George, took up my glass, and raised it. I could see his eyes were not focusing very well, but the flames caught his attention.

I said, "A drink to our agreement!"

He pulled his eyes away from the flaming papers, picked up his glass, slopping a bit onto the tablecloth.

"To our agreement!"

He lifted the glass to his lips and drank.

"This is the blood of the sacred white turkey, who sacrificed herself that we might know the truth!"

I put down my glass, took up a slice of turkey from the platter and stepped close to him. His eyes were very glazed now, but open, the pupils so dilated that there was no distinction between iris and pupil in this dim light.

"Observe! This is the body of the sacred white turkey who sacrificed herself that we might know the truth. Eat this in memory of her."

I broke a piece off the slice.

"What *is* this?" He demanded. "This is—this is—" He was still coherent enough to be outraged. He tried to stand up but weaved on his feet and fell back into the chair.

"This is the ceremony of the white turkey," I declared and I shoved a bite of turkey into his protesting mouth.

He drooled the bite out the corner of his mouth where it clung. I pressed it back into his mouth, held it closed. He chewed, obedient as a child, but when I dropped my hand and stepped back, his face hardened. He started to stand and sat back.

"What is happening? What did you do?"

He lurched up, caught his foot on the leg of his chair, and half turned. At that moment, Stella flung the white turkey from the opening pantry door into his face. White wings beat about his face as the turkey struggled against the string still binding her legs. Stella's voice came loud and angry from the pantry behind George.

"I am the spirit of the sacred white turkey! I am the holy spirit of the sacred white turkey! You dare to reject my body and blood! You will obey the pact you have made, that you have sealed with my blood and my body!"

The turkey herself had nothing coherent to say. She gobbled furiously, flapping at George, catching his shirtfront in the talons on her legs. George screamed and swatted at the turkey, who had now broken the strings binding her feet. George's chair went over sideways, the turkey on top of him.

"Obey the sacred white turkey! Keep the promise you made, or you will suffer the consequences! Obey the sacred white turkey!" I thundered the words at him, as he crawled, the angry turkey now following him, pecking at his legs. His shirttail had escaped from his jeans; his jeans had dropped a couple of inches as his knees crawling along the floor pulled them lower, exposing the crack of his buttocks. The turkey's beak pinched his bare flesh, and he screamed again, and I thundered again, "Obey the holy spirit of the sacred white turkey!"

"I will, I will," he hollered. Finally, he reached the washstand, got hold of a leg and pulled himself half up, the turkey now attacking his arms, his face. He flung open the door and half fell onto the porch, picked himself up, and tumble ran across the yard, yanked open his car door, and clambered in. Stella and I watched out the window.

Seconds passed, a minute while he dug his keys out of his pocket. The turkey sat on the bottom step of the porch, gobbling her anger. The Cadillac roared to life, jerked into gear, and backed across the yard, much too fast. Then it flung forward and out of the yard, catching a corner of the gatepost with a sickening thud and then a shriek as a long strip of chrome ripped loose from the driver's side. The engine roared but seemed to go nowhere very fast. He must have had one foot on the accelerator and one on the brake, stopping his own progress. Suddenly the car lurched forward, then it stopped, then it wandered from side to side down the driveway until it passed through the outer gate and disappeared over the little hill between my driveway and the main road. For a few minutes more, we could hear the roar of the engine in the distance, going away.

I looked at Stella. She looked at me. We burst out laughing. We could not stop. We sat on the floor, and we laughed until Stella got the hiccups, and that made us laugh more. Finally, stomachs hurting, we stretched out on the floor. At last, minutes later, I sat up and pulled Stella up.

I went to the door and looked out.

The turkey sat on the bottom step, still outraged.

14 Stella

All of those events that happened the summer of 1963 when I turned thirteen seem like yesterday, hard to believe it was forty-five years ago. Since then I've become an adult, married, had children and now grandchildren of my own. It has taken all of those forty-five years for me to come to some understanding of what happened, but even so, there are things I still don't comprehend.

Hazel's ceremony scared George Wanbli into leaving us alone, but it was the gossip that put an end to the scheme of stealing lease money. Hazel started it with the story she told Ruby and Pearl, and that story went through the gossip chain until everyone heard that Elias Villiers and George Wanbli were stealing everything from land to USDA commodities, the latter they were supposed to be storing in some cave they had dug out at He Dog Lake to sell to white people. Never mind that there wasn't any cave big enough to store more than a cheese sandwich, that there was no way to transport stolen stuff out of He Dog Lake without everybody on Rosebud and Pine Ridge knowing about it, that except for those big three-pound blocks of cheese that we all loved, most of the food commodities were so awful that we Indians only ate them when we were starving, so why would white people buy them, and a thousand other good reasons for not believing such gossip. For Hazel and me, it was enough that George Wanbli's and Elias Villiers's reputations had been tarnished, because in the election held that November, Elias lost. Without him in power as tribal council president, with George scared of retribution from the spirit world, Johnson Powers and Robert Grey and Mary Denison couldn't skim any more money off Indian land lease payments. Especially not since Ed Lately was elected as tribal council president, an office that he held for two consecutive terms, the only person in the history of our tribe to manage that feat.

You'd think that Hazel would have been content to know that she had stopped that graft, would have felt some sense of personal satisfaction, but she didn't seem to.

For weeks after the ceremony that scared George, she was not herself. Always self-sufficient, matter of fact in her speech and actions, not given to thunder in the mouth without lightning in her hands, she became more so—quieter, withdrawn. When people came to ask for her help with health concerns—a child with a lingering cough, an old person with joint ailments, a horse with a deep cut that wouldn't heal—she compounded her herbs into remedies; she wrote out the directions for their use. But people asking for help with spiritual matters was another matter altogether. She refused their offerings, sent them to other medicine people, even to the priests at Holy Rosary Mission a few times. Once a person that she had originally refused spiritual guidance told her they would bring her twice their original offering. She flew into a rage and threw them off the property. Eventually people stopped asking her for that kind of advice, and even people seeking only medical cures went elsewhere. The income after a year of this—both in money and in kind—dried up. We lived on what we could grow and the lease money payments. Even though they went up considerably after Wanbli and his people stopped skimming, it was still not enough. We did without, patched already patched clothes, and hoped that the food we put up from the summer would last through the winter.

I asked Hazel several times why she wouldn't do ceremonies anymore, why she wouldn't give spiritual advice, but she never answered me. She pressed her mouth into a thin line and walked away from me, as if the answer had to be contained, as if it was a secret and the telling would end the world.

The turkeys saved us. That second spring, the white turkey and her female offspring from the previous years hatched out forty-seven more babies, and most of those lived and grew into good-sized turkeys. That fall, Hazel and I killed and dressed them and sold them to white people in Jackson who preferred fresh turkeys for the holidays instead of shipped-in frozen ones. We ate what we couldn't sell, saving enough to produce more for the next year, and they did, in ever increasing numbers, every year for three more years. But we never killed the original turkey, the white hen turkey. The fourth year after she had come to us, she disappeared. One evening in April she was there when I let the turkeys and chickens out of the coop in the morning, but she wasn't there to be shut in that evening. Hazel and I looked for her everywhere, thinking maybe she had gotten caught in a wire fence and couldn't get loose, or had been hurt by a stray dog or a coyote, but we never found her alive or dead, not so much as a feather. She was only gone. None of the ten hens we had kept for brood hens hatched babies that spring. They laid not one egg.

One week later, when I went out to let them out, the chickens ran squawking for the feed, but no turkeys came out of the coop, and when I looked inside they were all in a corner, piled together, all dead. We could find no reason for their deaths. There had been no signs of illness, no molting of feathers, no running off of the bowels. Nothing. The night before, they were fine. The next morning they were dead, as if they had collectively willed their hearts to stop. Hazel would not dress them for us to eat. She said they probably had died of some disease, not safe to eat.

I didn't believe it. I thought they mourned their mother, grandmother, the white turkey, and had committed ritual suicide, although I didn't know how they had done it.

Hazel was worried, I knew, about what we would do without the extra money and extra food that the turkeys had provided, but a little while after the turkeys had all gone, she got a letter in the mail from a cousin down in Lincoln, Nebraska, who worked for the university. It was the 1960s, you know, and that was the time when anything to do with Indians was suddenly popular. We hadn't all died off or disappeared into the sunset, but sometime around 1966, people noticed that we were still around, and *interesting*. The cousin said that the university wanted someone to teach Lakota language, something that the cousin could not do. She had a few words left, she said, but once she said *pilamaya ye*, she was pretty much done. Would Hazel consider coming down to teach?

Hazel laughed, but when she found out how much they were willing to pay her to teach something that came as natural to her as breathing, she stopped laughing.

That's how come I finished my growing up in a city; that's how I came to get a college education, to marry, not a Lakota man from the rez, but a Creek man, a student at the university, and to move to California with him where my kids were born, and my grandchildren, too.

Hazel pretended for my sake that she was happy in the city, happy away from the land, but I always knew she took the job so she could take care of me. It was worse in the spring when the milkweed bloomed and the meadowlarks sang. She grew silent then, closed herself into the house as much as she could, and I knew she was remembering, remembering picking wild plants, mixing her herbal remedies, listening to the mating calls of coyotes in the night. She never went home again, not even for Sun Dance.

I never sold the land, nor will I ever. Descendents of the Olsen family still lease it from me, people that I visit every year along with Avril Lately and his family and others when my kids and I go home for the Sun Dance.

Hazel never told me why she stopped practicing as a spiritual healer, but I've always thought that she felt she had committed some kind of taboo, that the fake ceremony she performed to scare George Wanbli was a perversion of both her own traditional beliefs and the Christian ones that she professed not to believe in. She believed that she had meddled with ceremonial practice for reasons that were not appropriate, and that if she tried more ceremonies, the results would not come right, that they might bounce around and harm her or the people for whom the ceremonies were performed. Her penance was never to practice again, even though her original intentions were good and pure. Eventually, I think she lost faith in any spiritual practice at all. She never thought of the white turkey as I did, as so many other people did, never came to believe in its magical powers.

The turkey came to us from nowhere, provided us with the answers we needed if only indirectly, with practical economic necessities of food and money when we were desperate, and when we were no longer in need, she left and took her remaining offspring with her, in death. Or maybe not. I don't know. Hazel never believed in the holiness of the white turkey; she said the world had enough myths, good ones, and didn't need a new one that wasn't true anyway. But I know that white turkey was *wakan*, in the original sense of the word—something that cannot be explained. The appearance of the white turkey, the miracles I believed in as a child, the disappearance of the mother turkey, the death of her offspring, all of that runs from me like a phantom, disappears around a corner, and when I follow and look around that bend, nothing is visible but the breeze stirring a light dust and a few fat pigeons pecking at the ground.

IN THE FLYOVER FICTION SERIES

Ordinary Genius
Thomas Fox Averill

Jackalope Dreams
Mary Clearman Blew

Reconsidering Happiness:
A Novel
Sherrie Flick

The Usual Mistakes
Erin Flanagan

The Floor of the Sky
Pamela Carter Joern

The Plain Sense of Things
Pamela Carter Joern

Stolen Horses
Dan O'Brien

Because a Fire
Was in My Head
Lynn Stegner

Tin God
Terese Svoboda

Lamb Bright Saviors
Robert Vivian

The Mover of Bones
Robert Vivian

The Sacred White Turkey
Frances Washburn

Skin
Kellie Wells

To order or obtain more information on
these or other University of Nebraska Press
titles, visit www.nebraskapress.unl.edu.